SKINWALKERS

THE UPRISING

THE FINALE

A Novel by

Monica L. Smith

To submit a manuscript for our review,

email us at

<u>submissions@majorkeypublishing.com</u>

Dedication

I would like to dedicate this book to the ladies who gave me the idea of writing a book about Skinwalkers. Although I have changed a lot of it to suit the needs of this story, it was because of Rebecca, Ashley, Sharon, and Micah that I created this book.

I gain a lot of knowledge from each one of you and have even borrowed your names. From the deepest depths of my heart to its surface, I want to say thank you for all your support, your input, and your guidance.

Previously….

Gethambe

I knocked on Bullet's chamber door because it was time for us to make our move. I knocked several times but didn't get a response from him or Ashley. Normally I wouldn't intrude on their personal time, but we needed to get moving. So, I cracked opened the door and yelled his name.

"Bullet! We need to get moving, the sun will be up shortly."

I heard some moaning, so I figured he was still knee deep in Ashley. He needed to pull out and get to moving, so I walked in the door. I could see that Ashley was still sleeping but she was in the bed alone.

I tapped her on the shoulder and woke her up. She opened her eyes and smiled at me. No matter how many times I see this woman, I realize that I love her more and more every day.

"Good morning beautiful," I said, kissing her on her forehead.

"Good morning," she answered. "I have news."

I looked at her and laughed. "I don't know if I want to

hear any more news from you."

She laughed and then proceeded to tell me that she was with child.

"Lilith visited us last night and blessed us with our child. She did the same favor for Bullet that she did for you," she told me.

I was happy for them, but it pained my heart. I was trying to put another baby in Ashley myself. I figured that all her children would be by me.

"Where is the happy father?" I asked.

She looked around the room and was stunned that he wasn't still in the bed with her. I eased her mind by telling her that he was probably washing up and getting ready for the day. I told her that I would go and find him while she got dressed. I kissed her on the forehead and told her congratulations again.

I left Ashley in her chambers to get dressed while I looked for Bullet. When I was unable to find him on my own, I solicited the help of my Canine Crew. Although we searched every nook and cranny, we could not find Bullet.

When Ashley arrived in the conference room, I know she could feel the thickness in the air. She began to scan the room and to her dismay, Bullet wasn't in attendance.

"Lilith!" she yelled. "Samael!" she screamed. "Where are you?"

Samael shimmered into the conference room alone and tried to avoid eye contact with Ashley. But she walked right up to him and demanded that he tell her where Bullet was.

"This is not my cross to bear. I cannot tell you where he is. His secret is his alone," he said as he shimmered away.

"I can't worry myself with this right now. We need to go get Serenity and end this foolish war," Ashley said angrily.

I know that Ashley's heart was hurting because she couldn't see Bullet's fate or figure out what he was hiding from her. But she did a good job of covering up her pain.

I quickly went over the plan and we all knew what we had to do to break our daughter out of her prison. We all morphed into our beast and ran at top speed to the edge of the Winslow line to where the hotel sat on the old Route 66.

Half of the crew flanked the left side of the building while the other half of the crew flanked the right side. My father Jabri and I went straight to the front door and walked right in. On the bottom floor there were regular humans working. They looked at us with skepticism, but we figured it was because we were totally naked from where we shifted back into our human form.

"Excuse me, Mrs.," I started. "We were robbed, and they not only took our money but our clothing as well. Can you help us?"

The ladies all laughed at us but measured me against my father. This must have pissed my wife off because she came in the front doors like Shera. As her hands flung wildly, the doors flew opened. As she sashayed her way into the lobby, she tossed the humans left and right.

"I don't have the time or patience for this bullshit," she snapped, going to the elevator and pressing the button.

We didn't say anything to her, but we did follow her lead. They had her baby and she was going to retrieve her. On the elevator I heard her cursing to herself. I could hear her call out Bullet's name, but I couldn't make out the rest of the conversation because she was speaking in tongue.

When the elevator doors opened to the penthouse suite, Ashley didn't even look around for the Siberian Tigers, she stepped out of the elevator and commenced to whooping ass. I looked at my father and he looked at me. We shrugged our shoulders and shifted into our beast and joined in the fight.

I was fighting the ones that were running in from the staircase while my father was fighting those who were protecting the kingpin. In the midst of fighting, I caught glimpses of Ashley and a huge male Siberian tiger rolling around the living room. I feared for her safety but couldn't catch a break from the ones that were coming up from the lower floors.

The fight evened out when Rouge and the rest of my crew arrived. The penthouse was filled with sharp teeth and long claws. You could hear the loud howls and the deep roars as we fought till the death. I was ripping these beasts apart, tearing the skin from their bodies. But they were inflicting just as much pain on me.

I had gashes on my body that were spilling blood like a steadily running faucet. But even with the wounds that I had sustained, I continued to fight violently to save my daughter's life.

When I was able to catch a break, I looked over at Ashley who was pulverizing the large tiger. She was throwing spells, switching between her cat and her wolf, she was tossing him around the room like a rag doll until we all heard a loud voice yell, "CEASE."

We were all paralyzed. The only movement in the room was from Ashley and a much older Serenity.

"I have grown weary of the fighting. It stops today. I cannot be forced or persuaded to open Pandora's box. So, go home Lucas and take your pride with you. And if I see you in my next life, even than it would be too soon."

Serenity snapped her fingers and our bodies were freed. She looked around the room and then back to Lucas. "You have exactly twenty-four hours to leave this land or I will rip your spine from your back as I did my mother."

If he didn't realize her strength, he did now. He bowed his head and limped away from her presence with his crew close behind him. As we all began to shift into our human form, she spoke again, "Clothes," and we were all fully dressed.

She looked at her mother and told her that we needed to get to Alexandria so that she could say her final good-byes.

"Good-bye to who?" I heard Ashley ask.

Serenity didn't answer but waved her hand and teleported all of us to Alexandria. As we stood at the gates, we noticed a crowd gathering at the temple. Ashley immediately raced to it, pushing people out of her way. I ran behind her because I knew this couldn't be good.

When she reached the steps, there lie Bullet's body. She walked slowly up to him with tears falling from her eyes.

"We can beat this," she said to him.

"Not this time, Mon Cheri. I gave my life to protect our children's," he said.

"When?" she asked sniffling.

"When I asked the witch to place a spell on the portal. Her price to protect my family was my life."

"You should have waited," she cried. "We could have found a way."

"Don't cry my love. I will see you again," he said with his last breath.

We heard the loud drums of Anubis as he came to collect Bullet's soul. As the spiral swirled and the ground opened, Anubis appeared. He extended his hand and we saw as Bullet's spirit rose from his body.

"Can we offer another life for his?" Ashley cried.

"A deal was signed in blood. A favor for the protection of his family. This is a debt that can only be paid for by him," Anubis answered.

Serenity stepped forward and cupped her hands together in front of her.

"Precious jewels," she spoke.

Her hands were instantly filled with the clearest diamonds in the world. She gave them to Anubis and begged that he walk with Bullet to the gates of Heaven.

"No need for gifts, he is guaranteed a generous life in the eternity realm." Then he descended into the ground with Bullet's spirit.

Serenity and Ashley had the body brought into the temple and the priest prepared it for the ceremony. Once he was dressed in his royal attire, the Canine Crew carried his body to the Nile.

They placed his body on the royal ship that I had built for him. With tears in their eyes, Serenity and Ashley kissed him one last time as the Canine Crew gave the ship a gentle push. As it started to float away, we recited the Serenity

Prayer;

God grant me the Serenity to accept the things that I cannot change;

The courage to change the things that I can;

And the wisdom to know the difference between the two.

Living one day at a time; enjoying one moment at a time,

Accepting hardships as the pathway to peace;

Taking, as He did, this sinful world as it is,

Not as I would have it;

Trusting that he will make all things right,

If I surrender to his will;

That I may be reasonably happy in this life;

And supremely happy with Him,

Forever in the next.

AMEN

As we finished the prayer, the archer aimed his bow high toward the sun and shot his arrow. It flew like an angel and landed on its destination. As the sun began to nestle itself behind the snowcapped mountains, the ship burst into flames.

It was then that it began to thunderstorm.

Serenity stood strong, but Ashley fell to her knees in

the water. Following suit, both tribes took a knee and bowed their last bow to a great king.

"A part of him will always be with us," I whispered. "We will love his children and talk to them daily about the great deeds their father did for his people."

"It's not fair," she cried. "It's just not fair."

I didn't try to move her. I allowed her to sit there in the water until she could no longer see his ship. Nobody stood before Ashley, not even the children of the pack or pride.

Today, I lost a good friend, my children lost their father, and my wife lost her second husband.

Although this fight is over, the war has just begun. I made a vow to myself that I was going to revenge my friend's death by killing the Mad King Abrey and finishing that battle with the Siberian Tigers.

Like a wise man once said, "I'm living to fight another day."

~~~~~~~~~~~~~~~~~~~~

Chapter One

Ashley

It's been a couple of months since Bullet's death, but my heart still aches as if it just happened yesterday. Since his funeral, I have confined myself to Achacmenid. I cannot bring myself to visit Alexandria because I'm not ready to face the reality that I will never see Bullet again. I truly loved him and everything about him. I loved the way he cared for Serenity and always called me, Mon Cheri. I loved the way he put his family first and his needs last. I even loved his relationship with Gethambe and how they fussed at each other constantly. I just truly loved him...everything about him.

Gethambe has been strong since Bullet's passing. But I know that he is hurting too. They had become close and Gethambe had begun to value his presence. Although he would never admit it aloud, he cared for Bullet deeply. He had accepted him as my second husband and his brother. Yeah, Gethambe constantly rode Bullet's ass, but that was his way of showing him that he cared. Like real brothers, they fought over everything from traditions to women.

And not to mention Bullet's relationship with

Serenity. He was there for Serenity her entire life. She knew him as her father before she knew Gethambe. Her bond with him was unbreakable. They were close; closer than what she is with her biological father. Bullet had a way of making her sunrise and her sunset; he was her reason for smiling.

As I sit in my chambers and try to hold back my tears, I rub my stomach. Inside of my womb, my husband's seed is planted and growing slowly. This pregnancy isn't like the other ones, because I am hardly showing, and I believe that there is only one child inside of me. My heart breaks knowing that Bullet won't be here to see his child being born into this ratchet world. But it also warms my heart to know that he will be looking down from the heavens as I give life to his heir.

I heard my door open and when I looked up, I saw the love of my life looking at me. His eyes were soft, filled with love and concern. "Thinking about Bullet?" he asked.

"Always. There hasn't been a day that has gone by that I don't," I confessed.

"I think about him a lot too," he replied, walking over to sit on the bed beside me.

"I just don't understand why he didn't tell us what he

was doing. Why didn't he wait before making such a drastic decision?"

"Because he loved his family. All of us. And he did what he felt that he needed to do to make sure that we were all safe. Ashley, that is what a real man docs for those he cares for," he explained, holding my hand and planting a gentle kiss on the back of it.

"He was a loving husband and a wonderful father," I murmured.

"Yeah, he was a good wife and loving mother," Gethambe joked, making me laugh.

I hit him softly on his shoulder and said, "You know you loved him."

"I wouldn't say love. But his feminine ass grew on me just a little bit."

He wrapped his arm around my neck and pulled me close to him. Gethambe placed his hand on my tiny baby bump and rubbed my stomach in a circular motion.

"It's really small," I told him. "For me to already be fourteen weeks, I am barely showing."

"I've noticed. It's taking it longer to grow for some

reason. Maybe we will have Serenity see if she can hear its voice to make sure the baby is alright."

"Why wouldn't it be?" I questioned. "It would be two-thirds wolf and only one-third human."

"True. But nothing about our children is normal. Zira, Malik, and Dion proved that point," he smiled. Since their arrival, they have been inseparable. And we have noticed that Zira doesn't speak to us verbally, everything is through telepathy or the boys speak for her. We haven't figured out if they are gifted like Serenity because they haven't shown us if they have any type of power yet. They tend to play together like normal human children – with the exception that the boys don't allow too many people around Zira. Not even other cubs or pups.

Gethambe was right. All of our children were odd in a way. Serenity somehow became more powerful than me, Zira wouldn't use the verbal language, and Malik and Dion were overly protective of their sister. Not to mention, Dion and Malik also spoke in the ancient language, Aramaic.

"On another note, we have a couple of things that we need to handle," Gethambe said, looking at me with desire dancing in his eyes. It's been a while since we were intimate, and I know he was craving my wetness. But he knew the rules and he knew that he couldn't have any of my yummy sweetness.

"No. Not while I'm pregnant with Bullet's child," I laughed.

"I don't do pussy punishment," he huffed. "If I want that pussy, I'm going to take that pussy. If I feel the need to shove all this dick deep into your womb and tap Bullet's son on the head...I will. And there isn't a damn thing you can do about it."

"Whatever," I replied, blowing off the notion that he would even try my patience. "What else do we need to talk about?"

"That simple Simon nigga we found wondering around your domicile. He said that he is your ex-husband and keeps demanding to see you."

"William?" I gasped.

"Yeah. I think that is the name he gave Rouge. We have kept him locked away in the holding cell for over a month. To be fair, with all the shit we have going on, I forgot about him until Rouge mentioned it to me today."

"Oh my god. Is he okay?" I panicked.

"Why are you worried about this weak ass sissy bitch?" Gethambe asked as he pulled away from me. He stood up and his eyes turned cherry red and his heart became filled with jealousy.

"It's not what you think," I tried to deescalate the situation.

"I'm going to tear your little boy toy to shreds and distribute his body around the four corners of the earth so that you cannot find him again!" he yelled.

"Babe, you're not thinking clearly," I said. But Gethambe wasn't listening to me as he swiftly exited my room.

"You think I'm going to share you again with another man? Ashley, you have me all the way fucked up!" he barked; hitting the wall with his fist as he rushed to the holding cells. Quick on his heels, I followed him down the hallway and tried to calm his beast.

"No, Baby. William is my past. We were married and divorced before I knew anything about you or this life."

"So, now you're telling me he knows what my wife's pussy feels like?" Gethambe's tone was serious and harsh.

"Are you fucking kidding me right now?" I asked, trying desperately to keep up with his swift pace.

Gethambe was pissed but I knew that his anger had been misplaced. He wasn't mad that I had a life before him. He was pissed that Bullet was no longer with us and we were on the brink of war with the Siberian Tigers. His anger right now was just a cover for all the stress he was dealing with.

"Rouge. Juice. Get prepared because Gethambe is raging out and headed in your direction." I warned them telepathically.

As we made our way through the dimly lit halls, I could see that Gethambe was slowly transforming into his beast. I could also hear him yelling in his head about how he was going to rip William to pieces for trying to come and lay claim to me.

"Fellas, he's coming in beast mode!" I informed them.

As we arrived, Rouge was still in his human form alongside Juice. The rest of the Canine Crew that they had with them had morphed into their beast. And judging by how pissed Gethambe was, there weren't enough of them to hold him back. Rouge needed a couple hundred more soldiers or Serenity.

"My nigga. He's human, man. I understand that you're hurting, but this is not the way to go about healing your pain," Rouge said in a soothing, soft tone.

Gethambe's teeth and claws were extended and his body was in an attack stance. He was snarling with saliva streaming steadily from his mouth. He shook his head a couple of times as if he was trying to snap himself back to reality, but it didn't work, and he slowly inched forward.

"Freeze," I whispered, trying to stop him in his tracks. But while pregnant with Bullet's seed, my powers were not strong enough to hold him back. I was unable to stop him.

"Dude. Don't do this," Juice pleaded.

Again, he shook his head a couple of times but continued to inch forward. And as Gethambe got himself into position, he leaped into the air. Before his body came crashing down onto his soldiers, I heard, "Peace, be still."

I looked around to see Serenity standing behind us.

Her hair was blowing wildly, her eyes were a beautiful hazel color with hints of green, and her skin illuminated a gorgeous mocha tone. Her voice was so soft and angelic that it alone could soothe the savage in the beast.

She walked over to her father who was hovering over his loyal soldiers and said, "Lay easy, big guy, and rest." His beast slowly descended and landed softly on the floor next to her. Serenity sat on the floor next to her father and wrapped her arms around his neck. "Rest. This is not the fight that was meant for you."

It was a heartbreaking moment to watch Serenity console her father. She had tears swelling in her eyes, and the beast allowed his tears to fall from his.

As Gethambe shifted back into his human, Serenity used her powers to clothe him as well as the other soldiers that morphed back into their human form.

"Serenity. Can you teleport your father to our chambers while I check on an old friend?"

"Yes ma'am." She replied. "But before I do, be kind to William. You cursed him with leukemia and the doctors have told him that he only has a couple of months to live.

Although the human doctors can't heal him, you can. Find it in your heart to forgive him then let go of all the anger that you have rooted deep in your soul. I know his devious ways created a darkness in your core but remember that you can't get into Heaven with a hardened heart."

I walked over to my daughter and kneeled beside where she sat on the floor with her father and asked, "How did you become so smart?" Then I kissed her on the jaw and made my way to the holding cell door.

"I love you, Momma."

I turned and smiled at Serenity and said, "I love you more. Now take care of your father while I deal with my past."

With a wave of her hand, they shimmered away. I opened the door and found William sitting on the bed. Because I am a queen, I wasn't allowed to be with him alone, so Rouge and Juice accompanied me into his cell.

"Ashley. What the fuck is going on here?" William asked, getting up from the bed.

"My Lady, motherfucker. You will address our queen as, My Lady," Juice grunted angrily.

"And what the fuck is he referring to? Queen? My

Lady? Your name is Ashley."

I could sense Juice and Rouge were getting revved up. They felt that William was being disrespectful to me, but in all honesty, he didn't know our ways or traditions. He had no clue about this world and my new life. The last time he saw me, I was just – Ashley.

"William. My life has changed in a way that you would never comprehend," I said, sitting on the bed.

"Okay…Mrs. Queen. Do you mind telling me what the fuck is going on here? Why I was kidnapped in the middle of the night and brought here to this desolate place and held against my will? I have been locked up like a common criminal for so long that I don't even know how long I've been here."

I looked around the room and found it to be quite exquisite. He was provided a king-size bed with plenty of decorative pillows and a plush comforter. He had nice, clean clothes, a private bath with a jetted tub, a television, and gourmet food prepared for him daily. I don't think prisoners have such fine amenities.

"Why are you here, William?" I questioned.

"Because I want us to work things out. I want you to come back to me," he confessed. As he reached over and touched my hand, Rouge was on him within seconds, bitch slapping him – knocking the saliva from his mouth.

"Keep your hands to yourself," he ordered.

"Rouge!" I yelled out. "This is not how we treat our guest."

"I meant no disrespect, My Lady. But he is not worthy enough to touch you," Rouge explained. I loved how smooth his voice was, even when he was being a jerk like Gethambe.

I snapped my finger and a cloth appeared in my hand. As I leaned into William to wipe his mouth, he jumped backwards away from me.

"You don't have to fear me. I will not hurt you," I ensured him. Then I looked at Rouge and Juice and said, "And neither will anyone else."

They bowed their heads and moved backwards to the door. Then I directed my attention back to William and asked him again, "Why are you here?"

"I left my wife in hopes that we could rekindle our relationship. Since we have parted, nothing in my life has gone as I planned. I finally realize that you complete me," he admitted.

"William, there could never be a you and me again. I am married…with children. And I'm pregnant as we speak. My life has become complicated and has changed in a way that you would never understand. I'm not the same Ashley."

"And I'm not the same William. I grew up and now I'm ready to accept responsibility. I don't care that you have children by another man. I can be their father and we can raise them together."

As he said those words Rouge and Juice started to laugh hysterically. I ignored their childish behavior although I understood the joke.

I turned my attention back to William and said, "I will always love you, just not in the way that you're asking me to. I love you as a friend; nothing more. I have a family and a wonderful husband here. This is where I belong. With people who are like me. Not in the human world with you."

"Here you go again talking in riddles. The human world?" he asked. "Have you gone crazy and think you're from Mars or some shit like that? If you need psychiatric help,

I know someone."

I couldn't explain to him what I wanted him to know. So, I looked at Rouge and nodded my head. Within seconds, he was in beast mode and walking slowly up to William. When William saw that Rouge had changed into a large, snarling wolf, he leaped from one side of the bed to the other. Juice was tickled pink and couldn't stop himself from laughing as William cowardly hid on the other side of the bed.

When Rouge shifted back into his human, I whispered, "Clothes." I stood up and walked to the other side of the bed and kneeled beside William who was shivering uncontrollably. "As I said before, my life has become complicated. I have evolved into a higher being. I live in a world that you don't fit into. There could never be a me and you again," I smiled.

I still loved him, just not in a way that could fulfill his needs. And even if things weren't as they were for me, I wouldn't go back to William. Not after all that he has done to me. I have become accustomed to being treated like a woman instead of someone's ATM or part-time lover.

I stood up and extended my hand to him. Reluctantly,

he grabbed my hand and stood up too. As I held his hand in mine, I said a healing prayer that removed the leukemia from his body and rejuvenated his manhood. When I finished the prayer, I advised him that he would be fine and that I hoped that he would find peace within his heart and be blessed with more children than what he prayed for.

Even after I removed the curse that I had placed on him so long ago, he still wanted to stay here with me.

"You don't belong here, William."

"I don't have anywhere to go," he explained.

"William, what are you running from?" I questioned.

"Responsibility," Juice barked.

"Nah. He's running from honesty and commitment," Rouge joked.

"Loneliness," William answered. "I don't have a woman to share my life with and no family. And to add insult to injury, my loving wife disappeared with our child and the money from our bank account. You know my history and how I grew up in an orphanage. Ashley, I'm alone. You are all I have left."

With those words falling from his lips, the compound

alarm sounded. We were under attack and I had no time to deal with William's shenanigans. Gethambe and Serenity came rushing into the holding cell and warned me that we needed to get to Alexandria.

The Siberian Tigers didn't heed Serenity's warning. Instead, they stayed around until the weather cooled where they were better equipped to mount an attack on Achaemenid.

"Open the Portal of Life and get your mother to safety," Gethambe ordered.

"What about the human?" Serenity questioned.

"Leave him here with me. I will dispose of him," Juice announced.

Serenity knew that if she would have left William in their charge, he would be crucified for being in the wrong place at the wrong time. So, she cupped Williams cheeks in her hands, looked into his eyes and said a quick compulsion spell, "I'm sending you to Cancun where you will open a beachside bar and grill. You will forget about this place and only remember the good times that you shared with Ashley. You will always love her, but your conscience is cleared because you split on good terms. You will never come looking for her; you will move on and find happiness with someone else." Serenity then removed her hands and opened a portal. He looked back at me as if he was confused but walked inside the swirling ball of light.

"What about money?" I asked. "He said he doesn't have any."

"He has what he needs," she smiled at me. "Everything will be waiting for him when he arrives in Cancun. He will know where to go and what to do," she assured me.

As we heard the alarm sound again, Serenity summoned the Portal of Life and took me by the hand. Together, we flew through the portal at lightning speed and landed in the one place I wasn't ready to return to. I was home in Alexandria where I had laid my second husband to rest.

"Are you okay?" Serenity asked, watching me as I stared toward Bullet's chambers.

"Yeah," I answered. "I had to face my fears sooner or later."

"Well, know that you don't have to face this alone. I will always be here with you."

Although I could hear my daughter talking to me, I

was pulled to my late husband's bedroom door. When I opened it, I was overwhelmed by his scent. So much so that I collapsed.

~~~~~~~~~~~~~~~~~~~~

Chapter Two

Gethambe

It was a cold and dark evening with the sun setting swiftly behind the mountains. There were no sounds to be heard, at least none from this realm. But I knew that the devil was dancing with pleasure because this night would bring him plenty of lost spirits. Once captured by the soul reaper, they will be forced to either join his army of demonic soldiers or dance with the flames in his pool of sin. But I also knew that the keepers of Seventh Heaven were waiting for the fallen soldiers of the Canine Crew that were dedicating their lives to maintaining the peace and balance within this land.

With my family safely behind the walls of Alexandria with Serenity and Rouge, I released the predator that hid deep within me. My beast had begun to crave the flesh of the Siberian Tigers. I, along with my clan, lusted for the taste of their blood. I only had one thing running rampant through my mind and it was – murder, death, kill.

Stewart grabbed his team and made their way out of a secret exit. They would attack the tigers from the back and keep them from escaping. Joker and Juice took their armies and would be attacking Lucas's clan from the east and west. And I would take a fourth team and hit them head on.

As the other three teams got into place, I sounded the horn to have the gatekeeper open the gates. As we walked out; shoulder to shoulder, using our shields to form a wall of protection, my eyes were fixed on no one other than Lucas.

"So, you have to hide behind your shields? Are you scared to face me?" Lucas yelled out.

With that, the shields parted, and I stepped forward. Immediately, my crew closed their ranks, reinforcing the steel wall behind me.

"I fear no man or beast," I replied; my voice could be heard for miles.

Lucas walked slowly toward me and I walked slowly towards him. As we came face to face, my blood began to boil with rage. I wanted to rip his heart from his chest and chew it up and spit it out like chewing tobacco.

"Look. Why should we fight? All I want is for you to hand me Serenity. Once she gives me Pandora's box, I will leave," he smiled at me deviously.

Hearing him saying my daughter's name lit a fire deep

inside my body that water could not extinguish. He enraged my beast so much that my canines appeared, and my claws extended. I was breathing heavy and the hair on my neck stood out like sharp knives. He had truly fucked with the wrong man.

"So, you're so much of a bitch that you need a golden box to help you become a great king? Get the fuck out of here with that bullshit!" I replied.

"I am a great king. A true leader among my people. We are not domesticated house animals that have a master to tell them what to do and when to do it. We live by our own rules while you and your people praise an Almighty that you have never had the pleasure of laying your eyes on. Look at us," he said, using his hands to point at his people. "Then look at yourself."

"Your people are the very definition of savages. You run around like a primitive group of pussycats scavenging for power that you have not earned. You rape the land of its natural resources in hopes that it will reward you with wealth and prosperity. And you want to cheat your way through life and steal an ancient relic to help you dominate other realms.

Do yourself a favor and take your pathetic army home before you have no one to rule," I laughed. "Better yet, slit your own throat and save me the trouble."

But I could tell that Lucas had no intentions of backing down from this battle. He was willing to sacrifice every life there to get what he wanted. His clan wasn't fighting for a cause, they were being used as pawns to elevate Lucas's position. And that was fine with me. I had every intention of killing him anyway and then going after Abrey for the pain that he caused my wife.

I sniffed the air, extended my tongue, and pointed my ears upright to analyze my competition. With my senses sharpened, I could sense the fear that his body harbored. I locked my eyes on his frame and saw as it shivered slightly, letting me know that he knew this wasn't a battle he could win.

Not only could I smell the fear in him, but in his clan as well. Knowing that we were about to demolish them made my dick thump with excitement. I raised my arms and expelled a hideous howl, notifying all teams to move forward with their attack.

Uhmp…thump…uhmp! The sound of my forces

moving forward toward the enemy rang out like the nineteen bells in the bell tower at Christ Church in Dublin. I remained stationary as Lucas ran back to his front line and began shouting orders.

I simply held up my fist and then extended my four fingers, pointing them toward Lucas and his crew. Seeing that, my elite clan of killers began to run forward as they shifted swiftly into their beasts. I stood strong and steady as their large bodies ran towards the enemy, making my hair whoosh forward from the wind swirling around my body. Within seconds, they rushed past me and infiltrated Lucas's first line of defense. Blood immediately begin to spray high into the air like a fountain and pooled on the ground beneath their paws.

I watched them like a hawk as they ripped the Siberian Tigers apart like rag dolls. My clan dismembered their limbs and made large gashes in their bodies. My heart danced excitedly as I heard the cries from the enemy clan as the scent of their blood filled the air. It sounded like a seductive love song that elevated my passion for death.

I kept my eyes on the terrified bitch that hid himself

behind his troops. I watched as he scurried about his crew, pushing them in front of himself to save his own skin. He had to be the biggest pussy that I had ever laid my eyes on. How could his people ever look up at him as a leader when he used them as a human shield to protect his own life? It amazed me that he was as weak as a newborn deer fresh from its mother's womb.

With Stewart, Juice, and Joker moving in, they were surrounded. As I nodded my head, the catapults were pulled out from behind the gates of Achaemenid and loaded. I held up three fingers and counted down to a closed fist and the restraining ropes were cut, making the arm forcefully spring forward. As it flung the fire-charged payload through the air, my clan knew to move out of the way as it landed throughout the Siberian Tigers formation.

As their bodies burned, they ran aimlessly around and screamed in horrifying pain. One by one, bodies fell onto the heated sand, illuminating the ground with sunshine yellow, burnt orange, and scarlet red flames.

Lucas was running his hands through his hair with a look of confusion on his face. He paced frantically as he looked at the bodies on the ground, the incoming forces from all sides, and the air assault of burning arrows and huge stone balls. I felt deep in my heart that he knew that he had been defeated. The only problem was, I hadn't even begun to fight. I was just a spectator to the ongoing events.

With the last few remaining soldiers, I watched as he tried to motivate them to fight back. He was yelling words of encouragement and beating his fist against his chest. Although I couldn't hear his exact words, I could tell by his gestures that he was trying to reassure his clan that victory for them was on the horizon. And as they roared loudly in unison, they charged toward my direction.

I raised my arm and twisted my hand back and forth signaling my second line of defense to ready their swords and step forward. Moving as one unit, they pulled their swords from their belts, took one step forward and steadied their battle stance. I slowly pulled out my Bae, extended one leg with my waist slightly twisted, and held her horizontally above my shoulders with the sharp edge pointing forward.

As they charged toward my clan, I swung my sword swiftly, slashing the necks of my enemy. As I inched my body forward, I twisted and turned my body with military precision, cutting and slashing any of the enemy clan that ran in my direction. Tiger after tiger that I encountered, I shoved my sword deep into their bodies and released their souls. I was so focused on my mission that I didn't even see their bodies as they hit the ground. My body moved quickly, like the speed of light, as my sword swung gracefully, like a soft melody. When I stopped swinging Bae viciously, I noticed that there was only one person left...Lucas.

I looked at him with a heinous grin on my face. With my sword pointing downwards to the depths of Hell, my body decorated with his kin's blood, I was bathing in the victory that we had just received.

"Bring him to me," I ordered; my voice was calm but triumphant.

Stewart and Juice escorted him into my presence where again, we locked eyes. This time, I didn't smell the faint scent of cowardice, but the strong aroma of regret.

"I will still never bow to you or praise your God like a servant boy," he snapped.

"You must have me mistaken with that bitch who spat

you from her womb," I laughed. "You don't tell me what you will or will not do, you ungrateful mongrel. Be happy that I still allow you to have breath in your body."

"If you think I should be grateful that you are allowing me to live for the moment, you are sadly mistaken. Take my life and give my soul rest. Otherwise, I will continue to cause you and your family unnecessary heartache...every chance I get," he vowed to me.

"Is that a threat, pretty princess?" I asked.

"No. That is a promise," he answered.

His sarcasm irritated me, so, I lifted my sword and hit him in the head with the butt of it. Although I didn't hit him hard enough to knock his stupid ass out, I did hit him hard enough to make the skin on his forehead part like the Red Sea.

He just didn't know how much he made my dick harden with power. Unlike him, I have clearly displayed my strength, my knowledge of military strikes, and my exquisite leadership capability. But still, this little pussycat wants to egg me on. How cute.

"Take him to the holding cell and gather our injured. I will call on Serenity to heal our wounded and have the priest pray over our dearly departed before we send them into the afterlife."

As I made my way to the gates, I had an odd feeling that someone was watching me from a distance. The feeling was so strong and eerie that I stopped dead in my tracks and searched the land for this ominous entity.

"The aura that you sense is that of Abrey. He is the right hand of Lucifer himself. The Mad King is charged with leading his demonic army," Samael said as he shimmered in to view.

"He has an ass whooping on layaway," I snapped.

"He is not one to take lightly, young king. He has been around for many years and has led many battles. He loves killing just as much as you do. Before taking him on, if I were you, I would allow Serenity to take a trip to the spirit world and let her learn what must be done to bring peace back to these lands.

"So, are you saying that I cannot handle him on my own?" I questioned. Just knowing that he thought I was weak pissed me the fuck off.

"I'm not saying that a battle against the Dark Prince

cannot be won. But your daughter can give you a victory without the loss of thousands of lives," he explained, bowing his head to me. That was something that Samael had never done before.

"What needs to be done?" I asked him.

"Serenity needs to take a spiritual journey to learn her destiny. She needs to find a guardian or witch with old magic to help her pass through the spirit world to the Holy Realm where she will be able to see her future. Only the Almighty knows how to close the portal to Hell."

"How dangerous is this journey?" I asked. Samael never told anyone the whole truth. He got his thrill from being a mischievous demi-god.

"She will need an escort. I recommend that you find Pax. He is older than you think and has seen more than he speaks about," he explained.

"The last time I saw him, he was ripping his wife's head from her body and running out of the conference room with a broken heart," I huffed; as we walked into the golden-gates of Achaemenid. I then signaled for the gate-keeper to close them behind us because I was in no mood to take on a second battle at this time.

"You can find him at the Lion's Den, young king. Since the sad departure of his wife and the depressing news about his daughter, he has been there drowning his sorrows in the bottom of the whiskey bottle."

"You want me to depend on a drunk to care for my daughter during a journey into the great unknown?" I said, my voice filled with disbelief. I had to stop walking and look this demi-god in his eyes to see if he really meant to say that crazy ass shit.

"Regardless of his current situation, Pax is an excellent commander-at-arms. He has stood beside many kings and has won more battles than I can count. He is like the Hercules of your time. This man is strong, disciplined, patient, courageous, and extremely loyal to his king, tradition, and people. You will be a fool to send Serenity on this journey without him."

"But I have Stewart, Juice, Joker, and Rouge. And they all carry the same traits as Pax, minus the alcoholism."

I could see as Samael's eyes reddened and his body glowed an eerie color of gold after my last sentence.

"What are those children compared to a highly decorated soldier like Pax?" he snapped. "They are nothing more than mere puppets in a play, doing whatever you tell them to do without hatching a plan. Yes, young king, you were able to beat Lucas, but I can guarantee that you won't be so lucky going against The Mad King. Not even with the powerful Serenity. There is so much more that you should be worried about besides Pax's drinking problem," he hissed before shimmering away.

Hearing the seriousness in his voice gave me cause for concern. I have learned that when his words became harsh and slick, he knew more than what he let on. He often tried to refrain from telling one too much about the future because he didn't want to sway it one way or another…unless it was to his benefit.

When Lucas was secured and all of our injured and dead were taken care of, I tasked Juice and Joker with locating Pax and bringing him home. They had orders to use whatever force necessary to get him inside the gates of Achaemenid, as long as he wasn't hurt.

I left Stewart in charge of Achaemenid while I made a

trip to Alexandria to check on my wife. Before the battle started, Serenity spoke with me telepathically. She stated that Ashley had passed out when she opened the door to Bullet's chamber. It hurt me deeply because she warned me that she was not yet ready to face her past, but I sent her there anyway.

Serenity has the power of dream-walking. She can enter your dream and guide you out; waking one up from a coma. But she stated that every time she has tried to enter Ashley's dream world, she is pushed out by her sentinels, the entities that Ashley created to challenge all newcomers and keep them out.

As I flew through the Portal of Life and stepped into Alexandria, I made my way to our old chamber we shared together before leaving. I opened the door to find my wife resting like Sleeping Beauty. What made the scene so heartwarming was, while she laid there sleeping peacefully, one single ray of sunshine slipped through the cracks of the temple and illuminated her body. Serenity was laying in the bed beside Ashley, singing softly to her and rubbing her belly that had grown since I had seen her a couple of days ago.

Then, as I looked more at the scene of the room, I

noticed that Dion and Malik were standing on each side of the bed and Zira was standing at the foot. They had their hands in a praying position with their heads bowed. Malik and Dion were chanting the Serenity Prayer while Zira remained perfectly still and quiet.

Serenity sensed my presence and slid slowly out of the bed to ensure that she didn't interrupt the triplets as they continued to work in unison. She slid close to me and began to whisper what was happening.

"Zira doesn't have the gift of verbal communication. Although she has a beautiful, sweet voice, you will never hear her speak any words aloud."

"Is my daughter a mute?"

"No. She talks to people telepathically."

"What are they doing?" I questioned. I was afraid that Serenity was about to tell me that my wife was crossing into the afterlife.

"They are a power of three. Zira is the strongest, but her powers are cut in half without the support of her brothers," Serenity smiled.

"What the fuck," I gasped. Because my wife is

partially demi-god, she has blessed all of our children with mythical powers.

"So, what are they doing to her?"

"Zira, with the help of Malik and Dion, is tricking the sentinels that Mother is using to block me from her dream subconscious. Once they find her, they will help her heal her broken heart by escorting Mommy to Valhalla."

"Valhalla?"

"Warrior Heaven," Serenity giggled. "The people here don't believe in the traditional Heaven and Hell as you do. They believe that there are many parts to Heaven and many parts to Hell."

"And once she is in 'Valhalla', what will happen?" I inquired.

"She will see Daddy Bullet again. She will get to say good-bye and then her heart can begin to heal."

"Don't tell me that even in death he will get to fuck my wife," I huffed.

Serenity snickered at the jealousy that filled my body. Yeah, I was used to him dicking down my wife while he was alive, but I don't think I could deal with her fucking a ghost.

"No, silly. They will talk and then they will release each other's spirit. And if she chooses to accept another man as her second husband, she could do so once her son is born."

"Why would she want another second husband?" I questioned. "She has me, Gethambe?"

"Because it's the tradition of Alexandria for the queen to have two husbands," she whispered.

Before I could digest the information that was just given to me, the room was overwhelmed with a bright white light that expelled from Zira's eyes and mouth. Her small body levitated into the air along with her two brothers. And there they stayed, suspended into midair as we watched Ashley's spirit rise from her body.

Like Ashley, our children's spirits were pulled from their bodies and all four floated up and disappeared. This had to be one of the scariest things I have ever seen. And when Rouge opened the door and entered the room, seeing all their bodies suspended in air made his bottom lip hit the floor.

"Whatever happens, we must not disturb their bodies, or their spirits will be lost in purgatory," Serenity warned. Although she didn't notice, I saw how she looked at Rouge.

She paid attention to his presence about three seconds too long, letting me know that he was a man of interest to her.

She then waved her hands and stone guards appeared inside and outside of the room. They had the bed surrounded, along with the door to the bedroom and the door to the temple.

"Only the three of us can enter," she whispered into the air. Hearing their orders, they stomped their staff on the floor and positioned their body in a battle stance.

"How long will they be like this?" I questioned.

"Until she finds the strength to let Daddy Bullet's spirit go," Serenity explained, as she ushered us out the door.

Her advancement was a little more noticeable now because where as she pushed me along, her arm was intertwined with Rouge's. As he escorted her out the door, the exchange of affection between them was evident. The way she looked at him made me realize that my baby wasn't a baby anymore; she had become a desirable young lady.

Although I wasn't mad, I was concerned. Everyone knew that she was going into heat; her scent filled the air for miles.

~~~~~~~~~~~~~~~~~~

Chapter Three

Abrey – The Mad King

After watching that hideous battle between Lucas and Gethambe, I shimmered back down into the Underworld. I had other shit that I needed to worry about…like my daughter that Lilith tortures on a daily basis.

I have been watching over my seed since her spirit had been denied entrance into Heaven. Her happily-ever-after was snatched from her when Samael gave her as a gift to Lilith. It's true that her devious deeds against Ashley and Serenity awarded her a life of servitude, but nobody understands the fact that Gethambe wronged her first.

I wasn't surprised though. I knew that her reign as queen would fall. It had been written and foretold before Lana was even born. This had to happen, and she had to fall into despair before she could truly appreciate the power she would inherit. Once she takes her place here, she will become a force to be reckoned with as well. All she needs to do is allow me to upgrade her skills to where she would perfect her new-found evilness. She has it in her, I just need to show her how to release her beast once she turns into the demon that has been chosen for her.

Lana wasn't ever meant to be a topside queen, she was meant to be the wife of Lucifer. We both have watched over her since the day she was born. Her intense beauty captivated the Dark Lord, her wickedness stole his heart, and her essence hypnotized his mind. He craved her. But due to her being under the protection of the Almighty, he couldn't have her. Funny how the tides have turned. Now she was his for the taking. And once they are married, she can help me obtain a powerful relic that will help me dominate the realms. I too will become a God.

I waited patiently for Samael and his entourage to leave and go topside. Hell was not a place that his whores like to visit. It reminded them that they too have been condemned to a life of destitution. Although they lived a lavish lifestyle here, they hated knowing that their souls would always be tied to Hell. But since Samael took them under his wing and married each one of them, they were sort of protected, especially Lilith.

She was the original wife of Adam and they lived in the Garden of Eden. They were the beginning of humanity.

Although Lilith only gave birth to one child, she is still considered the mother of us all. When she ran away from her true husband, Adam, another woman was created from her blood. Eve was blessed with the ability to create and give life, but it was Lilith's blood that sourced her being. When Eve was created from Lilith, she too was cursed with the treacherous traits of seduction and deception that led to the destruction of the Garden of Eden.

Being the great father that I am, I allowed Lilith to have her fun with Lana. I needed them to break her spirit and show her how it feels to be powerless. Doing so will teach her to respect the power that she will yield being the Queen of the Damned. Also, being punished day in and day out will harden her heart which will make executing any and all orders without emotions possible.

Because I loved Cherish and respected my Dark Lord, I released Lana to her mother and watched as they lived a privileged, pampered life on the earth. Cherish allowed that sorry ass husband of hers to teach Lana how to give respect without being respected; how to humble herself, doing unto others as you will have them do unto you, and how to be seen and not heard. Cherish and Pax are the reasons why my daughter is as weak as she is.

Although my heart is cold, and I lack emotions, there is a warm, soft spot for my daughter. Unlike her brother, I know that she will eventually embrace the dark side. When she gives herself to Lucifer, she will no longer lust for power because she will hold a lot of it in her tiny, frail hands.

I slipped into the luxurious home of Lilith and her sister-wives to make contact with my seed. As I walked down the hallway, I found my daughter on her hands and knees being fucked savagely by Samael as Lilith and the sister-wives looked on. Lana was screaming as he pounded irately inside her tiny frame. He had her hair wrapped tightly around his one wrist and the other hand imbedded deep into her waist.

As Samael rode my daughter hard, rage built up in my body. But this wasn't the time for me to mount my attack. Instead, I allowed him to finish his dirty deed as Lilith and her crew egged him on.

"Make the bitch cry!" I heard Lilith say.

"Choke the deceitfulness from her body," Na'amah laughed.

"Teach this treacherous bitch a lesson, Samael!" Agrat bat Mahlat joined in.

But I didn't hear anything come from Eisheth Zenunim. She watched as her husband brutally raped Lana; she didn't join in with her sister-wives, but she didn't stop Samael either.

When he finished his heinous hate crime against my daughter, he stood up and waited patiently for his wives to run to him and suck his dick clean. All of them were devouring Lana's cream from his semi-hard dick. As they finished, and he redressed himself, he used his foot and kicked Lana to the floor.

"My home isn't clean, you worthless bag of walking skin," he snapped.

Lana apologized to Samael as tears raced down her face. She immediately picked up a nearby toothbrush and began to scrub the floor. My heart shattered into a million pieces as I looked at my daughter. Her clothes were worn, her body was covered in black and blue bruises, and with the repeated rapes…her soul had been conquered.

When Samael and his demon wives finally shimmered

to the topside, I slowly walked over to where Lana was and kneeled beside her.

"Lana," I whispered.

She didn't answer or look in my direction. Instead, she continued to scrub the floor like a mindless drone.

"Lana," I repeated, laying my hand on top of hers.

She stopped scrubbing and jumped backwards away from me. "Sssshhh. The mistress doesn't like noise. You have to be quiet...very, very, very quiet or she will beat you," she whispered back to me, placing her finger over her lips. Then she crawled back into her position and continued to scrub the floor. "Must keep cleaning," she giggled softly as tears continued to stream down her face and her body trembled slightly. "No rest for the wicked," she quietly chanted to herself.

"Baby girl," I murmured, using my finger to pull her hair out of her face and back behind her ear. "Look at me."

Lana ignored me and continued to make small circles with the soapy toothbrush on the floor. "Must keep cleaning...cleaning...cleaning. Must keep cleaning to keep the beast away," she sang.

I placed my index finger under her chin and pulled her head around to where she could see me. As she fixed her gaze on to my face, I could see the confusion in her eyes.

"It's me. Your father," I smiled at her.

"No," she laughed mysteriously. "My father is Pax Yazzie. And because I turned my back on the people he loved, he has turned his back on me. You're nothing more than a figment of my imagination. Sent here by Lilith to trick me," she said, sitting up on her knees and hugging herself. Tears were now pouring from her eyes as her body swayed back and forth to the beat of an unheard drum.

Lana began to look around the room and then up to the ceiling. Without warning she yelled out, "I'm not falling for your tricks, Lilith. Not this time." Then she began to laugh hysterically as if she had gone mad.

It was then that I was able to really look at my daughter and see how her appearance had altered drastically since arriving to the underworld. She was no longer that beautiful, graceful queen that I had watched over for so many years. No. Lana looked as if she had aged thirty or more years, she spoke in broken sentences, and she had lost her will to fight. Those evil bitches and demonic false god had tortured Lana so much that I wasn't sure if I could revive her spirit.

I stood up and my temperament became dark and furious. "That whorish, bitch of a mother lied to you. I am your rightful father. I am Abrey Klah, the rightful king of Alexandria and the Dark Prince of the Underworld. I am father to Bullet Klah and Lana Klah. And to be all the way honest, I am the first and rightful husband of Cherish Klah! Now, get up off your knees and let me help you, help us, reclaim our kingdom," I explained; my voice was loud and thunderous.

As the walls shook, Lana stood up and looked at me with a blank stare. It was if she was looking through me and not at me. Her body stood perfectly still, and her face displayed no emotions.

She wiped her tears away and stated, "If you are truly my father, and you are truly the Prince of the Underworld, then why have you left me here to suffer under the cruel hand of my captors? Why have you stood idly by and allowed Lilith and her family to torture my very existence….Father?"

"Because you had to be broken before you could be

fixed. And I couldn't tell you before now because of the deal that was made between the Dark Lord and Cherish. I may be powerful, but he is law here. I'm just the enforcer. But know that I have been watching over you since the day you were born," I explained.

Although I tried to hold up to the façade of the heartless bastard that killed for sport, at this moment in time, Lana was tugging at my heart. I had been denied being a part of her life, and now I held her very existence in the palms of my hands. It felt like holding a newborn baby.

Hearing me say her mother's name woke the true beast that lie dormant in her soul. "I hate that woman with a passion," she hissed, crossing her arms over her chest and sucking her teeth. "I hate her more than I hate that murderous bitch, Serenity!" she spat pure fire as her daughter's name fell from her mouth.

Without realizing my actions, I slapped the demons from her body and exorcised her aura. She had no right to talk about Cherish or Serenity in that manner. She didn't know her mother's struggle and how she was once nothing more than a common whore to the king and queen of Achaemenid.

63

Pax had told King Jabari that he desired Cherish. So, she was given to him as a reward for him being a loyal and faithful commander of the Canine Crew. King Jabari had even promised to make their first daughter queen and guaranteed them a plush life in the beautiful city of Edom. But when Cherish became pregnant and gave birth to a litter of sons, she made a deal with the Dark Lord for a daughter.

And Serenity was an innocent child in all of this. She didn't kill Lana's sons; Cherish's bargain with the Dark Lord did. If only she had a partial relationship with the girl, I could swoop in and play the caring grandfather and cypher all her powers and use it for our own personal gain. Yes, I would keep Serenity around because she is a part of me, but it's her power that I lust for more than a relationship with her.

"Don't you ever speak ill of your mother or daughter in my presence again. Family is family...regardless of their past," I scolded her.

She looked at me with hatred in her eyes and barked, "I hope her soul is down here burning in Hell for all eternity!"

Again, I raised my hand to the upper realms and rained it down onto Lana's face. She fell to the floor and blood streamed steadily from her mouth. She wiped it away and stood back up and looked at me with disgust. "You hit like a bitch. I've been socked harder by Lilith," she laughed. "Fuck Cherish and fuck Serenity!"

"You're in my realm now, you ungrateful heathen. And regardless of you being my daughter, I will smite you down to the depths of Hell where your mother resides if you don't show me some respect. There your soul would burn over and over until I feel that I am tired of hearing you scream in agonizing pain from the flames that will consume your flesh!" I warned Lana.

She was now analyzing her situation and I knew that she had underestimated my cold heart. I was just as ruthless and demonic as the Dark Lord himself. Family didn't mean shit to me unless they had something to offer. I cared for Lana...I did. But I cared more about the value she would bring to my life.

"As much as you would like for me to forgive Cherish, I just can't. I will never acknowledge her as my mother. Not even for the freedom that you offer to me. She has wronged me in a way I could never forgive. And if you resurrect her and allow that monster to get close to you, I promise that she will wrong you too. It's in her nature to be a manipulative bitch who uses what she has, to get what she wants. You would do better by asking me to forgive Serenity."

I turned my back to her and began to walk away. I didn't have the time or patience to listen to Lana's shenanigans. I couldn't care less if she forgave her mother or her daughter, I'm going to get what I want regardless. Lana didn't have to agree with me or follow suit, because her view on life would soon change once she dances with the devil.

"Wait. Where are you going?" she asked.

"To give the Dark Lord what he craves," I answered. "Must keep cleaning because there is no rest for the wicked," I taunted her.

"And what does the Dark Lord desire?" she questioned. "For me to suck him dry?" she hissed.

"You," I answered. "He has a deep desire for you."

She looked at me with hungry eyes. She was now beginning to see the light at the end of the tunnel.

"Yes, Baby Girl, you are who he has desired for years. No other woman has caught his attention like your aura has.

When I offer you to him, and you gain a piece of the Dark Lord, you will then help me obtain an ancient relic that I can use to transfer Serenity's power to myself," I smile devilishly.

"You can't take Serenity's power. She's untouchable," she yelled as I made my way to the door.

"For you to have been so smart, you are so stupid. You should learn more about your history before you open your mouth. But don't worry little moccasin, Daddy will teach you everything you need to learn."

"I hate when people call me stupid," she stated, stomping her feet like a young child having a temper tantrum.

"Maybe I should have presented this idea to a real queen. I could have easily molded Serenity to take over these realms instead of stealing her powers. She doesn't need the intense help that you require to reach her fullest potential," I laughed as I opened the door.

Serenity?" she asked; her voice filled with hatred.

"Yes. Serenity. The most powerful entity in the realms. Favored by the Almighty, The Elders, and the people of Alexandria as well as Achaemenid. Your flesh and blood that you tossed away like garbage. Yes. Serenity," I informed

Lana as I stood in the doorway.

It excited me to see some type of emotion from Lana. Her skin turned red, her eyes were refueled with jealousy, and I could smell the sweet scent of resentment spilling from her pores.

"That little whore killed me," she announced.

"Nah stupid queen. She beat the shit out of you and then ripped your spine from your body," I laughed. "She was the powerhouse you threw away. And even when she asked you for forgiveness, you stepped on her heart and erupted a volcano of built up anger. Way to fucking go, Mommy Dearest."

It was hard to believe that after Lana learned about how Serenity became one of the most sought-after deities in all the realms, she still refused to allow her daughter to become a part of her life. If Lana had been smart, she would have welcomed the opportunity with open arms and then used that girl to help her dominate the world. But it's too late now, she hates Lana as much as Lana hates her.

"Don't call me that!" she yelled.

"See, you have me just a tad bit confused, little

moccasin. I don't care about your temper tantrums or your feelings. So, as I heard Gethambe once say...know your role and stay in your place...stupid, dead queen," I said; my words were calm, smooth, and cold.

Lana lowered her head in defeat. Her tongue wasn't sharp or quick enough to challenge mine.

"Look, Lana. Instead of sitting around here throwing daggers at each other, why don't we just work together? You help me, I help you, and we will both get what we want...our teamwork could possibly conquer the realms."

She looked at me as if she had to weigh her options but ultimately agreed. I walked back to the door and gave her a hug and ensured her that I would be back soon.

"What should I do if Lilith and Samael return?" she asked.

"Exactly what you've been doing. Whatever they tell you to do."

She exhaled her breath as if hearing those words irritated her. But I gave her a little assurance that everything was going to be okay by saying, "Those bitches don't have nearly as much clout as I have in the Underworld. When the

Dark Lord needs something done, it's me that he calls on…not the Four Witches of Eastwick. The only thing that Lilith and her sister-wives are good for is fucking and sucking dick. And to be honest…Medusa's pussy is a lot tighter and her head game is to die for."

Lana smiled and looked around the room. She found the toothbrush that she had been using to clean the floor and assumed her position.

I leaned down and gave my daughter a kiss on the forehead and made my way out the door. The Dark Lord's mansion wasn't too far from Samael's house of horrors, so it only took me a couple of minutes to walk there.

As I walked through what seemed like Death Valley, I realized that Hell wasn't any different from any other realm. Yeah, the temperature here was elevated…by a lot, but when you become a part of the elite, Lucifer provides his crew with luxurious homes and fast cars. As long as you put in work, then the Dark Lord took care of you.

When I made my way to his house and rang the doorbell, I was greeted by one of his main whores. She pulled me in the door and into her arms. As of right now, Lei was the head bitch in charge, but she wasn't Queen of the Damned.

She gave me a kiss on the jaw and pointed to the sliding doors. I smiled at her and made my way over to Lucifer. This nigga killed me. His ass was laying out on the patio, smoking a blunt, and watching the pool of souls as they burned in a never-ending flame. As the many voices screamed out in agonizing pain, he was bobbing his head as if he was listening to a new rap song.

He looked up at me and pointed to the chair that was closest to him. Lucifer was tall with a muscular build, had dark skin, hazel eyes, and long black dreads. This nigga could pull any bitch at any time; even knowing that he's the devil himself, women fall at his feet for a few minutes in the bed with him. I admired that shit.

"Business or pleasure, my nigga?" he asked, passing me the blunt.

"Both," I answered and then took a long draw from it.

He smiled at me knowing that the pleasure part had to do with Cherish. But I'm sure him hearing me say business, piqued his interest as well.

"Business before bitches," he laughed, as I passed the

71

blunt back to him.

"Look. I know you're looking to add some new talent to your team," I started.

"Go on," he smiled, placing the blunt in the ashtray.

"You know Lana is here?"

"Yeah, she's Lilith's new pet? Funny, Samael was here earlier telling me how she has no clue on how to please her husband," he laughed.

I hated knowing that Samael was taking advantage of Lana in that manner but there was nothing I could say because it was approved by Lucifer. When you do wrong to one of our own, your soul is tortured in any way the owner feels fit.

"But she can be taught my Lord. You've been watching over Lana just as much as I have, and you know the hand she has been dealt," I explained.

"Go on," he said. I could see the twinkle in his eyes. He knew he wanted her; he just wanted to see what I was willing to give up for him to take her as his wife.

"All I want in exchange is for you to help me locate the philosopher's stone. I want to use it to transfer most of Serenity's powers into my being. I would leave her enough to use during a battle, but most of her energy would become mine," I smiled. "As a bonus, once I take what I want, you can have her too. You could use her to negotiate with the Almighty and elders or make her your second wife. Although she doesn't know it, she is able to visit Seventh Heaven whenever she chooses," I explained slyly.

Lucifer sat straight up in his chair and gave me his undivided attention. He knew what I was saying to be true. Serenity was considered the Almighty's greatest creation. It was foretold that she and her husband would lead their people in a victorious battle between good and evil. But, if her power was slightly diminished and she never had the opportunity to marry because we swiped her from the topside, evil would triumph.

"Serenity….Serenity…Serenity," he sang. "She would be a great asset here, even if she was only at half strength," he smiled, swinging his long dreads out of his face. "I could marry Lana, making her my queen, and kidnap Serenity, making her my princess. The three of us would be unstoppable."

"And all you want is for me to help you get the

philosopher's stone?"

"And allow me to rule six of the twelve realms as an equal," I whispered. "I will continue to oversee your demonic army of soul eaters, but I would focus a lot of my attention on ruling my kingdom with my wife."

After taking the blunt from me and taking a few seconds to think over my proposal, he snapped his fingers and a contract appeared. "And what about the pleasure?" he questioned; blowing a cloud of smoke out of his mouth.

"I want Cherish. Release her from the pool of sin and make her my wife."

"For real, for real my nigga?" he questioned. "You can have any woman your heart desires and you ask me for Cherish. Why would you even want to waste your time on that bitch?"

"Is it a deal?" I asked him. I then picked up the small knife that was on the table and slashed the palm of my hand.

"Deal," he answered, pointing to the contract and summoning Cherish's soul.

I placed my bloody hand on the contract. As soon as the deal was sealed with blood, Cherish and Lana appeared.

"Welcome home...wifey," Lucifer smiled. He was looking at Lana while licking his lips as lust danced in his eyes. He snapped his fingers again and her appearance became flawless. She once again looked healthy and elegant. "We will wed tonight, I can smell the egg within you that I will fertilize. I can see that you will give me a worthy heir; the son I desire," he told her as he looked deep into her soul.

"As you wish," Lana answered, bowing her head to the Dark Lord.

She was then escorted into the mansion while I took my bitch home to retrain her on how to be a good, loving, and obedient wife.

~~~~~~~~~~~~~~~~~~~

Chapter Four

Serenity

I had been spending a lot of time with Rouge; he makes me feel beautiful and wanted. He's not amazed with my power, but more so with my mind, body, and soul. Although he is so much like my father, he has a way of making my day brighten. I not only see my father Gethambe in him, but I can see the gentleness of my father Bullet in him as well. We are so compatible in so many ways and I feel that we were fated, but when I smell his essence, his scent is off.

As we entered Lucas's holding cell together for a routine investigation, I couldn't keep my eyes from examining Rouge's masculine physique. Without him touching me, I could feel every bulging muscle in his body. I became short of breath as I imagined him wrapping his massive arms around my small frame. I was gasping for air when I thought about him stealing passionate kisses from my lips. Being this close to him made my body shiver with want. I had become hypnotized by his demeanor and in love with his being. I don't know how it happened or even when it happened, but I woke up one morning and knew that he was the man for me.

"I can smell your leaking pussy," Lucas whispered. "You're coming into heat," he laughed.

"And what business is it of yours?" Rouge demanded to know.

"None," he answered simply. "Just know that once her sweet virginity is taken, she will not be able to open Pandora's box. Serenity will no longer be pure enough to accomplish that task. It will be then that all hope will be lost."

"Why are you so obsessed with Pandora's box?" I questioned. I then walked over to the fireplace and watched as he took a large gulp of bourbon from his glass.

He was so much different from my people, but I could see his past and realized why he was the way he was. For so many years he has been shunned from the Almighty's graces because of his beliefs. Because he doesn't worship or believe as we do, he was thrown away like garbage…forgotten…removed from our history books.

After analyzing him, my heart softened just a little. He was no different from me. His heart was kind, his reasoning was just, and his knowledge was vast. He deserved the respect that he fought so diligently for. His only problem was he was going about things the wrong way. But I could teach him, I could help him understand the ways of our people, I could even accept him as one of our own. Lucas could teach us a lot about his lost history.

"She asked you a question," Rouge reinforced.

Lucas didn't even acknowledge that Rouge was in the room. He looked up at me and said, "What are you doing here little kitten?" He was swirling his ice in his glass as if he was signaling me to give him more to drink.

I walked over to the bar and picked up the bottle of Kentucky Bourbon and walked over to him. He held his glass up as I opened the bottle and poured him a healthy helping of the dark liquid. He didn't look at me; his eyes were now fixed on the dancing flames.

"Lucas, why do you hate us so? We should be working together, not fighting and killing each other like savages," I said, as I kneeled beside his chair and watched the flames with him.

Rouge allowed me to take the lead. He knew that Lucas had a different type of want or respect for me. He knew that he would give me the information we needed without

Rouge having to beat it out of him. So, Rouge slowly backed away and took a seat on the bed and just watched as I pulled the information from him that we wanted.

He took a gulp from his glass and continued to investigate the fireplace as if he was watching a movie. I could tell that he was searching for the right words to say to me; the right story to recite in order to make me see things from his point of view.

"I don't hate anyone. I hate that you and your people act like slaves to a God you will never know. You run around like puppets and do his deeds without question…like mindless drones. Your people have been pets for so long that you don't know how to think for yourselves. And if *YOUR ALMIGHTY* took away your shifting abilities, would your people even know how to care for themselves? Live in the wild amongst their counterparts and survive?" he hissed.

I thought about the words he was saying and knew that his way of thinking was driven from hate of what happened to his people so many decades ago. Although I wasn't in agreement with him, I wanted to know more.

"You say that your people were once the protectors of

these lands. Why were you cast out?"

He took another large gulp from his glass and swirled the ice in its emptiness. I knew that he was telling me to refill it as if I were *HIS* servant girl. His lack of respect for women reminded me so much of my father. His arrogance excited me, and Rouge noticed it. But he sat there quietly and allowed me to continue with my questioning.

Doing as he wanted, I filled his glass with the bourbon and waited patiently for him to tell me the story of his life and of his people.

"The old history that has been erased for many years says that we are all derived from Maahes. He was the son of Ra and the feline goddess, Bastet. He was the original shape-shifter and the greatest warrior within all the realms. He was tasked with leading armies against Satan and devouring the demons that wreaked havoc within the realms."

"Maahes? I've never heard of him," I said. I have read through every book in Alexandria's library and this name wasn't   mentioned   in   any   of   them.

"He was imprisoned by the Almighty because his rage couldn't be contained," Rouge interrupted.

Lucas looked at Rouge in disgust and said, "Because he was removed from history. His soul is what is hidden in Pandora's box," he explained.

"Why would the Almighty lock him away if he was as fierce as you say?" I asked.

"Because he went on a murderous rage. My father told me stories about how he defeated this ominous god," Rouge huffed.

Lucas continued to stare into the flames as if it was replaying the past for himself as he told me about his forgotten hero. "Maahes fought continuously to maintain the peace and balance over the twelve realms. But it took a toll on his being. So, he took the Siberian Tiger, the wolf, and lion and blessed each of them with a piece of his heart. He gave the Siberian Tiger his strength and discipline. My people fought side by side with him, keeping the demons from escaping the Underworld and conquering any of the twelve realms. He blessed the lions with loyalty, agility, and courage. They were the protectors of the lands…a different type of lion was placed in each of the realms to keep order and protect that kingdom. And the wolf was blessed with knowledge, honor, faith, and integrity. Your people were our justice system…the peacekeepers," he explained.

"That still doesn't explain why the Almighty would erase him from history," I snapped. I was beginning to believe Rouge's story more than the lies that spilled easily from Lucas. I had to remind myself that he was a master of deception and would say anything to sway my view of his ways.

"Like Zeus, *your God* is a jealous god. And when the people of the twelve realms began to worship Maahes instead of the Almighty, he removed him from history and locked his essence away in a tiny box under the Great Temple of Alexandria. Because our loyalty lies with Maahes, our kind was expelled from these lands and the mountain lions became the protectors. History was altered because your God wants to be the only god," he explained.

"LIES!!!!" Rouge yelled out, standing up from where he sat quietly.

I looked at Rouge and smiled. He was so much like his father, passionate about his family and traditions. His eyes met mine and he knew that I was politely asking him to let me handle this. So, he sat back down but fixed his gaze on Lucas.

"So, what is it that you want from us?" I wanted to know. "I'm not opening Pandora's box because of your lost king."

"You will," he said simply. "Now that you know, and before the final war comes knocking on the walls of Achaemenid and Alexandria...you will go down into those tombs and open that box."

"I don't have any visions of another war," I said, standing up and looking down onto Lucas.

He looked up at me with sincerity dancing in his eyes and stated, "Because your sight is blinded by the Dark Lord himself. You are blessed with sight...that much is true. But not even you can see what happens in Hell. You need to take a spiritual journey, and let your ancestors guide you down the path of righteousness."

"What?" I questioned.

"A spiritual journey," Lucas responded, holding his glass out for me to add more ice and bourbon to it. As I grabbed the glass and walked over to the bar, my mind began to wonder. What if he's telling the truth about the shift in power between the species?

I placed a ball of ice in his glass and filled it to the rim with the bourbon and handed it to him. I crossed my hands over my chest and raised one eyebrow. I looked down onto him and said politely, "What is your end game?"

He chuckled as if I had just told him a joke. He swirled the ball of ice in his glass and gulped down his drink as if it was the last bit of bourbon in the world. Then he stood up from his chair and walked up to me. He was so close that his rich cologne smothered my senses. Lucas looked at me seductively and answered, "My end game is to possess the spirit of my king and marry the woman I long for – you. Serenity, you are the cure to this disease-infested place. I can show you how to use your powers to their fullest. Yes, you can yell out a couple of words and make people do what you want them to do. Yes, you can see a glimpse into the future. But if you give me the chance, I can show you what you are really capable of."

"At what cost?" I asked, falling victim to his slick tongue, amazing body, and captivating soft sage eyes.

"All that I would ask of you is that you release the soul

of Maahes before the war between Heaven and Hell begins. Unite me with him and allow me to help you rule Alexandria."

"Are you fucking kidding me?" I hissed. "I've told you once, I'm not opening Pandora's box…not even to release your deity. There is a reason that the Almighty felt the need to lock him away and there is nothing you could do to convince me that it was due to jealousy. My God isn't that petty."

Lucas turned his attention from me and focused it on Rouge. He walked over to him and said, "Take her to see Nola. You know her, and your father trusted her to take many of his people on a spiritual journey. Nola will show Serenity what she needs to see. Before I embarked on this battle, I visited with her. Although she shielded the face of the king of Alexandria, I could tell that the person in my vision was me."

"Nola is rooted with old black magic. She is a very deceitful person and sometimes alters one's vision to suit her needs. I would never subject Serenity to her treacherous ways," Rouge huffed.

"Nola is no more harmful than a pussycat. And if you don't trust her, send Serenity with an escort. Easy fix," he smiled. "But it would need to be a man who is skilled in battle…like your father. He is not only a great warrior, but he is well versed when it comes to malevolent women who are skilled in the art of illusion. Makes me wonder how Cherish was able to manipulate him."

"I can protect Serenity," Rouge snapped. He stood up and looked at Lucas angrily. I could tell by the tone of his voice and the position of his body that Rouge was ready to strike.

"She doesn't need your protection, toy soldier. She's a god. There's nothing you could do for her that she couldn't do for herself," Lucas chuckled. "You think that because you are the right hand to Gethambe, a boy king, that you're ready to walk in the footsteps of a man? Do us both a favor and go find your father before Hell breaks free."

Within seconds, I was standing between them. We were only here to gather information, not fight. But I must admit, with all the testosterone in the room, I could feel the cream within my sweet spot pooling into my panties.

"Mmmmm," Lucas moaned, as he licked his lips seductively and stared down at my sweetness. "Can you smell that, son?" he chuckled.

As Rouge's teeth began to protrude and his claws extended, I snapped my fingers and teleported out of the holding cell and into the conference room. As I wrapped my arms around his neck, I smiled.

I took my tongue and began to passionately lick one of his protruding canine teeth, slowly running my tongue up and down its length. Then I took the time to give the other one just as much attention as I gave the first one.

He wrapped his arms around my waist and pulled me close to him. Slowly, his beast calmed, and his teeth retreated along with his claws. Rouge started to shower my neck with soft and delicate kisses making my heart pound with want.

"I can't taste the sweetness of your love until I get the approval of your father," he whispered.

"We don't have to tell," I murmured.

"We don't, but I would. Your father is like a brother to me. I not only respect him as the king, but I respect the bond that we have formed over the years," he said, sucking lightly on my neck.

Every flicker of his tongue made desire race

throughout my body. Every soft kiss took my breath away and made me fall deep into ecstasy. And every time he slightly touched any part of my body, it made me cream in excitement. But as I inhaled his scent, I became confused and frustrated. Although he felt right, my senses said that he wasn't. However, I couldn't deny the attraction that pulled me to him.

"When are you going to talk to my father?"

"Soon. But right now, I want you to talk to mine."

Rouge pulled away from me and tried to reposition his manhood. Judging by the bulge in his pants, he was well-endowed, and I couldn't wait to feel him inside of me. I respected the fact that he wanted to wait until he spoke with my father, it showed that he was a gentleman. I just didn't know how much longer I could hold myself back.

When we gathered ourselves and grounded our desire for each other, I opened the Portal of Life. Together, hand and hand, we stepped inside the magnificent ball of swirling light and made our way back to Alexandria.

My father had been waiting for our arrival to see what we had learned from Lucas. He knew that if he sent me to talk to him, Lucas would spill his guts. Lucas wanted my wetness more than Rouge.

As we stepped out of the portal, we were still holding hands. My father noticed the small piece of affection we displayed, but he didn't say a word. I think he knows something, but he is waiting for us to come clean with our feelings.

"So, what did you learn?" he asked, walking toward the throne room.

"He wants Serenity to go on a spirit journey to find out her true purpose," Rouge answered.

"Nola?"

"Yeah. And you know that bitch can't be trusted," Rouge replied.

As my father sat quietly on his throne, I could tell that he was deep in thought. I could see the wheels of wonder as they twirled rapidly in his head. He wanted to know the truth as much as I did, but I knew that he wouldn't put my life in danger. I was strong, but even I could be tricked and misled.

"Where's Pax? Has he sobered up?" my father asked.

"I can do it, Gethambe. I can escort her through the

spirit realm and protect her from that witch's treachery. I love Serenity and would die for her," he confessed.

My father looked at him, stunned by his words. Although I was a woman, I know that he still saw me as his little girl. And as I looked at my father, who was staring hatefully at Rouge, I knew that I had to intervene.

"And I'm in love with Rouge."

"I have no time to entertain your childish crush – girl," my father huffed, and then turned his attention back to Rouge. "Have you defiled her?"

"Never, my nigga. I would never take what is not mine. The only thing I have ever stolen was her heart; as she has stolen mine."

"Excuse my behavior. My heart is heavy. We will revisit this when I am thinking clearly. But if she is to walk among the spirits, she needs to be escorted by someone who has visited there many times before. I need your father. Samael forewarned me of this moment, and I think its best that I take his advice."

"Juice, I need to see Pax," my father said to him telepathically. *"Please tell me that he has sobered up."*

"Funny that you ask about him, because we are coming through the temple doors now." Juice answered.

As the doors to the temple opened, I motioned for the stone guards to allow them entrance. I could barely recognize Pax. His appearance was that of an elder. He appeared to have aged significantly.

When he entered, my father rose to his feet and walked over to him. He stared at him for a moment before pulling him in for a hug. As my father held him close, Pax began to cry.

"It feels good to be back, although this is not my home," he said.

"My wife has fallen ill, and we can't go home until she recovers. I cannot move her body while she is dream walking," my father explained.

"How can I help?" Pax asked.

"By protecting my daughter as Nola sends her to the spirit world for answers."

"She cannot be trusted. Nola's allegiance lies with Lucifer not with the wolves," Pax said, pulling back from my father and walking over to his son. They gave each other a long hug before he turned his attention back to the situation at hand.

"That's why I'm calling on you. Lucas swears that Pandora's box doesn't hold the elements to destroy these realms, but his long-lost king, Maahes. And Samael feels like we are on the brink of another war, this time with the Underworld."

"Maahes? The god of war, protection, and weather? The first shape-shifter?" Pax questioned.

"So, you heard of this deity?" I asked.

"Yes. He was the first king that I was assigned to. He taught us the skills that we needed to have in order to protect these lands. Maahes is the brother of Lucifer."

"Get the fuck out of here!" Rouge laughed. "We have to go up against two super power demons?"

"Not exactly. Maahes was created to control Lucifer's lust for power. Because Lucifer wanted to plague the realms with hatred and darkness, the Almighty gave life to Maahes. His strength, wisdom, and honesty came from the demons that he devoured. The only problem was, he had a vivacious appetite and couldn't control his yearning for their blood. So, when balance was achieved, the Almighty locked him away," Pax explained.

"In Pandora's box?" my father asked.

"That, I don't know," Pax answered. "I'm willing to walk through the spirit realm to find out from our ancestors. But I ask that you send my son into battle with me. I have gotten old and this is something that he would need to learn to pass down to his sons."

"Agreed. What needs to be done?"

"There is a Hogan located just outside these gates. Serenity needs to cast a powerful spell of protection around it. While we are walking through the spirit world, we will be unprotected against any enemy forces that should try to attack us. It must be one that ensures our safety inside the Hogan from Nola and another one for the outside. When we summon Nola, she will alert Lucifer," Pax explained. "Serenity will need a spell from Eisheth Zenunim's ancient grimoire," Pax informed us.

"Why Eisheth Zenunim?" I asked.

"Because Eisheth is the first and most powerful witch within these realms. No other witch's power can compare to hers," Pax replied.

"If she is so powerful, then why can't she walk with us through the spirit realm?" I questioned.

"Although Eisheth Zenunim is loved here, you have to remember that she is still a demon and shunned from the Heavens," Pax explained.

"How do we get Eisheth Zenunim to fork over her grimoire?" I inquired.

"Simply by asking me for it," Eisheth Zenunim answered as she shimmered into view, along with her sister-wives.

~~~~~~~~~~~~~~~~~~~~~

Chapter Five

Lana

As the servant girls scurried about the house preparing my new home for the wedding, I sat quietly on the balcony of my room and looked over my new kingdom. Within a matter of hours, I was about to become one of the most powerful entities in the Underworld.

Before arriving, I had spent many hours in the various libraries researching anything and everything that dealt with my people, the mountain lions, demons, fallen angels, and of course – The Dark Lord. Who knew that all that unnecessary information would pay off for me one day?

I was giggling on the inside knowing that I would be his first wife and blessed with a third of his powers. The reason being is, he must cut my heart out of my chest and replace it with one-third of his. We will be bonded for eternity. Although I will never be as powerful as him, I will still reign supreme. The only way that my powers can be taken from me is if the Almighty himself comes down from the Heavens and removes my heart at Lucifer's request. But I wasn't worried about that in the least bit. I'd plan on being the best fucking wife in the world to him. I am going to fuck him often, bear his seed, and be as submissive as he needs me to be.

"My Lady," the servant girl said, bowing before me. "The Dark Lord wishes to have a word with you in the study."

I acknowledged his request and shooed her away. I sat there quietly for a few minutes longer taking in the beauty of Hell. Who would have thought that someplace so cursed could be so breath-taking? I didn't mind waking up as queen to this magnificent view every morning. I could get used to the constant pampering I would receive as Lucifer's wife. I could get used to just being myself without wondering if I am an embarrassment to my husband. I was ready for this moment; I was ready to rule Hell. I took one last glance at my new kingdom before getting up from my seat and going inside my new mansion to talk with my future husband.

As I walked gracefully through my new massive home, looking at the luxurious décor and expensive artwork, I found my way to the study. As I entered, I stopped just a few steps from his desk and bowed to show him respect.

"Nice," he grinned. "I like a woman who knows their

place. Have a seat," he said, pointing to the chair on the other side of his gorgeous cherry oak desk.

I know this is not the right word to use, but as I glanced at him, I couldn't help but to thank God for creating a being so gorgeous. I was smitten by his hazel eyes that often changed colors, his dark chocolate skin that had a seductive shine to it, his long, black dreads that he often let hang messy, and his muscular physique. How could the Almighty make something so rotten look so tempting?

"You sent for me, My Lord?" I questioned in a soft and pleasing voice.

"Yeah. I wanted to get a feel for you. See where your head is," he answered; sitting back in his seat and looking at me as want danced seductively in his eyes.

As his eyes ran rampantly over my body, I smiled pleasingly at him. Remembering how my father told me about how Lucifer has lusted for my sweetness for years, I decided to pull him into my essence and see how bad he wanted to taste my juices. I knew that it was going to take me some time to be able to flawlessly execute the art of seducing the Dark Lord, but the devil inside of me couldn't help herself from taunting him early.

Slowly, I unbuttoned the top three buttons on my shirt and used my hand to fan myself. "It's so hot in your office," I smiled.

Lucifer leaned forward and focused all his attention on me and the way I pretended to pant for air. "You know I want that? Come here," he demanded.

I stood from my seat and walked around to his side of the desk. He turned his chair to watch my body as I made sure to swing my hips seductively for him. I positioned myself between his legs and kneeled to my king.

"I've watched you suck Gethambe and seeing what a pathetic job you did tells me that you're not ready for this anaconda yet," he laughed. "Get up off your knees, your tongue is not what I desire right now."

I bat my eyes at my soon-to-be husband and smiled wickedly. "What does My Lord desire?" I asked.

As I stood up, he pulled me close to him and buried his nose in my sweet spot. He inhaled my scent and expelled an exciting growl. He used his hands to ease them up my legs and beneath my skirt. They were soft but very masculine, igniting a fire within me that has been extinguished for quite some time.

He skillfully located my panties and used his long, sharp claws to cut them on both sides. We both watched as they fell to the floor, then we locked eyes as if to say, what's next. He stood up and guided my body to sit on his desk. Lucifer than opened my legs and positioned himself between them.

As he wrapped his arms around my small waist he asked, "You will be my first wife. My only wife. There is no divorce here. Are you willing to give yourself to me?"

"I have no one. I have nothing. I am battered, abused, mistreated, and tossed away. Garbage is worth more than the life I am allowed to live. At least with you, I will have a title, a purpose, and a place," I explained, speaking my truth.

"You know I have to kill your soul by removing your heart the minute you say I do?"

"Yes."

"But I will give you a part of mine in return. Lana, we will be bonded for all eternity. Although there will be other women for my pleasure, you can only be intimate with me. At times, I may request your presence, but it will never be with another man."

"Are you trying to scare me away?" I asked him. Hell, I've never had a husband of my own so having to share the Dark Lord with other women wasn't anything that would push me away from him. I learned that it was only sex...nothing more. And if another bitch wanted to give me a break from pretending that this man is giving me the best sex ever...she can happily be my guest. I had other things, more important things on my mind.

"No. I'm trying to give you the opportunity to back out. Your father gave me your hand. You never said that this is what you wanted. I may be the Lord of the Underworld, and I may seem cold and cruel, but I do have a heart."

"Lucifer, I just want my happy ending. I want a man to love me, not mistreat me. I want a man to respect me, not beat or degrade me. I just want to feel wanted for once," I said, with one tear falling slowly down my face.

He wiped it away, pulled my chin up, and planted the softest, sweetest kiss I had ever felt on my lips. It was so in-depth that it took my breath away. What the fuck? Everything that I had ever read about Lucifer and Hell had been evil and bad. But as I see my new kingdom, I'm surprised by its beauty and Lucifer has been quite the gentleman behind closed doors.

"When you become my wife, I will love you. I will give you everything that you want and then some. I will never hurt you, but if I find that you are being deceitful or that you have allowed another man to enter or touch your body, I will take my heart back and you will cease to exist. Your soul will wander the realms without purpose. I am a jealous man and require that you cater to my every need without question. Here, you need to know your place and stay within the limits that I will set for you after we are united."

"As you wish."

He then sat down in his chair and parted my legs like a gynecologist readying himself to give me a pap smear. As he dipped his head between my thighs and flickered his tongue over my clit, I fell backwards onto his desk and deeper into euphoria. His tongue was so wet, soft, and enticing. With every stroke, he pulled me into his being. And every time he sucked and pulled on it, my blood warmed with desire. He made it feel so amazingly good.

"Uhm," I moaned, as I wrapped my legs around his neck and began to rotate my hips.

He came up for air and told me, "Your scent is tantalizing, your juices are stimulating, and I can tell that you are ovulating. Tonight, I will put my seed into you."

"Fuck!" I yelled. "Put your seed into me now!"

"After the wedding, My Wicked Angel. I cannot cum in you until your body has been converted over to the dark side," he informed me. "I just needed to make sure that we would make a good match. I thought Lei would be the one, but something about your wickedness outweigh hers by a long shot."

"Could it be my wolf?"

"You don't have your wolf or cat anymore," he confided in me.

I pulled my body up and looked at him curiously. "I don't have my wolf?" I questioned. I didn't give a fuck about the cat that lay submissive in my genes. The wolf was all I knew and had been a part of my history since day one of my existence.

"No, My Wicked Angel. You lost that when you died

and descended to Hell. And when I give you a third of my heart, you will take on the demon trait. And what type of demon you will become I don't know until it reveals itself to me after the ceremony."

I leaned down to him and cuffed his cheeks in my hand. I pulled his face up to me and licked my cream from it. When I was finished, he stood up and ran his hands up my silky legs. I scooted my body close to his and pulled him as close to me as I could. Slowly, I began to dry hump against his massive hardness, thinking about how good he would feel deep inside of my womb.

"Oh, Baby," he hummed. "I just want to see what it feels like. Can I just put the head in?" he begged.

"Say please," I taunted him, knowing that I was going to allow him to do it anyway. I needed to know if what Samael had said about me was true. When he found the need to rape me, he would say how loose I was, how inexperienced I was, and how he could understand why Gethambe needed the love of another woman. He said that I didn't have what it took to satisfy a man.

"Please, My Wicked Angel. Please," he begged, using

his long, wet tongue to seduce my neck. He was slowly running it up and down its length, arousing every nerve in my body.

"Just the head," I grinned mischievously.

He looked deep into my soul and shared a small intimate smile with me. Although I didn't look down at first, I could sense that he was holding a beast in his pants. Something long, strong, and magnificent.

"This is going to hurt. You're going to feel like you're a virgin all over again," he moaned. Then he pulled out his long, thick python and slowly began to push himself inside of my sacred garden.

As his tip touched my entrance, I held my breath and threw my arms around his neck. As he pressed gently, the pressure felt so painfully good. But I guess I wasn't wide enough for him to ease it into my body, so he slowly worked his hips, thrusting his manhood into my wetness.

"F-U-C-K!" I yelled. I felt like he was ripping me in half as the head of his hardness pushed forcefully inside of me.

"Awe yeah," he moaned, as he delved deeper. When

he was fully submerged into my sweet spot, he stood perfectly still and allowed his hardness to pulsate violently. By this time, I was trying to do that Lamaze breathing technique in hopes that it would lighten the throbbing pain.

"My Lord," I gasped. "You're quite large and this is slightly painful." No. The truth was he was enormous, and he was killing me.

"Sssshhh," he whispered in my ear. He still didn't move, but we were so close that our hearts were beating simultaneously.

When he felt my body relax, he pushed my body backwards onto the desk and leaned over to me. He took one hand and wrapped it securely around my throat while he used the other one to steady himself. Slowly, he began to thrust his hips, pushing in and pulling out of me gracefully.

Although I could barely breathe, I managed to say, "You lied, My Lord. You said only the head."

"Did you really believe that I would only put the head in?" he huffed, power-driving his hardness so deep into my wetness.

As he slow stroked me, everything inside my body

began to tingle in excitement. The more he enjoyed my wetness, the tighter his grip became around my neck and waist. I looked into his eyes to see them changing colors quickly; going from an enticing hazel to a seductive ruby red. His skin started off warm but quickly became as hot as the scorching sun. And the scent of whatever cologne he bathed in engulfed my nostrils and hypnotized my senses. Without trying, the Dark Lord had made me cum a river. Within seconds there was no pain, only a euphoric pleasure.

I wrapped my legs around his waist and relaxed my body. Matching his slow and harmonic pace, I swirled my hips on his hardness making him moan softly. I wrapped my hands around his wrist showing him that I was enjoying the fact that he was choking the ecstasy from my body.

For the first time, I wasn't being fucked by a man. The Dark Lord was making sweet, intimate love to me. I realized that he was showing me that he was capable of loving a woman and that I deserved to be loved. We both were filled with trickery and dishonesty, but we were beginning to find happiness in our deceitful ways...together.

As his hardness began to pulsate violently inside of

me, I could feel him pulling his manhood out of my sweetness. "My cum will eat up your insides," he growled, holding his hardness in his hands.

"How can I help you release?" I asked. "Teach me."

He looked at me with disappointment in his eyes and whispered, "Go find Lei. She's a demonic succubus that is immune to my semen. I cannot hurt her."

"As you wish, My Lord," I said to him, getting down from his desk and repositioning my skirt. I bent down to pick up my panties when he asked me to leave them there. I didn't question him, I only did as I was directed.

I approached the door and turned the door knob to feel Lucifer standing closely behind me. He was breathing heavy and feeling his breath on my neck sent shivers racing down my spine. I started to open the door when he placed his hand on it and closed it back. I turned around to look at him and became captivated by those alluring hazel eyes.

"Don't make me fall in love with you and then you do something stupid to where I will have to rip my heart from your chest," he said; his words were filled with emotion.

"I know what it feels like to be hurt. I wouldn't wish

that on my worst enemy…not even on Serenity."

He looked at me mysteriously and then asked, "Can you leave that pain behind you and move forward with making a life with me?"

"I hate her with every drop of blood in my body. I want to see her body swimming in the lake of fire as her flesh continuously burns from her skeleton."

"That is a sight you will never see. Serenity is enlightened by the Almighty himself. Let her go and give the son I am promising you all the love in your heart. I tasted you, I felt you, I see you," he said; his voice started out strong but before he finished his sentence it became soft and pleasant.

"For you, I will try," I smiled, leaning in to him and giving him a long and enduring kiss. As I pulled away, I sucked passionately on his bottom lip making his hardness thump aggressively.

He took his fist and slammed it against the door as he expelled a deep breath. "Go get Lei," he murmured.

I turned back to the door and twisted the knob with Lucifer leaning against my body. This time when I opened the door, he didn't move; he allowed me to walk out to go find the tramp that would suck and fuck him well. But I was okay with that.

I started up the steps to find Lei coming down them. I could see why he was so infatuated with her. She had to be one of the most beautiful women I had ever laid my eyes on. I stopped her on the steps and told her that Lucifer required her attention. But I had to ask her why she was condemned to a life of hell. I wanted to know who she pissed off.

"Aphrodite," she answered. "I became pregnant by her lover, Ares. She killed my unborn child and gave me to Lucifer as a gift. She is a very jealous and vain woman. If she wants someone, she does whatever it takes to get him." Her words were soft and kind, but most shockingly...forgiving. "I must not keep the Dark Lord waiting," she finished. "He is a very impatient man," she smiled at me, then walked away.

I made my way to my chambers and began to prepare myself for my wedding that was going to happen within a couple of hours. The first step to becoming the wife of Lucifer required me to bathe in a bath of virgin blood. And to my dismay, the servant girls had already filled the tub and were waiting patiently for my arrival.

When I entered the bathroom, I did what any good, submissive, wife-to-be would do. I stripped from my clothes, pulled my hair up into a sloppy knot, and stepped slowly into the thick, warm liquid. To prove that this is what I wanted, I dipped my head deep within the sunken tub and emerged victorious. I was ready to become, the Queen of the Damned.

<center>~~~~~~~~~~~~~~~~~~</center>

Chapter Six

Ashley

I opened my eyes and was immediately blinded by the rising sun. My body was naked, and I was laying on a bed of moss and lilies. The wind was lightly blowing, filling the air around me with the sweet aroma of dandelions and roses. As I sat up, I could see nothing but large trees and bluegrass fields for miles. I had an overwhelming feeling that I had died and gone to Heaven. What other place could make you feel that you have been wrapped in tranquility and blessed with serenity. I felt peace all around me. I felt love from the tip of my head to the bottom of my feet. I felt...at rest.

I stood up and looked down onto my body and realized that my belly had flattened. I was no longer pregnant with my husband's child. The one thing that kept me close to Bullet, I had lost. But for some reason, I wasn't saddened by this event. Something deep within me was saying that it was okay. So, I'm assuming that the child was saved before I died. Although I would have loved to hold him or her at least once, my heart told me that the baby was fine and blessed.

Feeling refreshed from my nap, I stretched, extending

my arms far up to the Heaven while my toes dug deep into the ground. As I began to walk through the tall, cold grass, I could hear children laughing. I scanned my surrounding area to find the little bodies that belonged to the soft voices, but I found no one. As far as I could tell, I was walking through this massive field, alone.

I did notice off in the distance a huge snow-capped mountain with smoke coming from it. Something was pulling me in that direction, but I was afraid. I would have to climb this enormous mountain and I had no clothes to protect me against the harsh weather that I would encounter. Then I remembered, I'm not pregnant so my powers should be at full strength. So, I whispered aloud, "Winter Clothes."

When I looked down at my body, I noticed that I was still nude. Then I heard the children laughing at me again. "Who's there?" I yelled out. "Show yourself," I demanded.

There was complete silence for a few moments and then she appeared. My God, she was the prettiest little girl. She had to be about fifteen with the shiniest red hair and cutest freckles. Her skin was a creamy soft tan, her eyes were emerald green, and her smile was devastating. Instantly, I became lost in her essence…she gave me the false feeling that I knew her, but I couldn't recall from where.

"Come here baby. Are you here alone?" I asked, running my hands through her silky red spiral curls.

She smiled graciously and then pointed behind me. I looked around to see two cute little boys. They too looked to be around fifteen years of age. They were both chocolate with these amazing, soothing blue eyes. They had long, black, silky hair and a stern look on their faces. I was shocked to notice that both boys had a tribal tattoo going around the upper part of their right arm. I was assuming that they were there to protect the young girl.

I felt a soft tap on my shoulder, so I turned around to see that it was the cute redhead that was trying to get my attention. The smile that she had on her face was so soothing. Her persona gave off an aura of peace and love. Being near her made me feel so safe and secure. It should have been the other way around, I should have made her feel as if she was wrapped in tranquility.

"I'm glad we found you," she said in a soft and comforting voice.

"Are you lost?" I asked her.

She giggled quietly as she continued to look at me. But I was concerned about these kids that were out here without parental supervision. Although this place was peaceful, I knew that there had to be some sort of danger lurking in the dense woods ahead of us.

"No. But you were," she answered.

I looked at her in confusion. I wasn't lost...but I wasn't found either. I had an overwhelming feeling that I had passed on to my next life. But I was okay with that. I knew that I would be reunited with Bullet and waiting for Gethambe to join us soon. We would be together again...one happy, dysfunctional family.

"I'm not lost sweetheart," I smiled at her. "I know where I am."

Again, the three of them laughed at me as if I had made a joke. Better yet, they were laughing at me as if I had made an ass of myself. I looked around my surroundings and noticed that the two boys were now standing close to me. They were looking at my nude body with curiosity.

"I'm sorry," I apologized. "I don't know why I don't

have any clothing on. Maybe we all go before the Almighty the same way we came into this ratchet world…naked and alone," I explained.

"You don't know us?" the lighter of the two boys asked.

"No," I answered. "Should I?"

"Yes," the darker boy answered. "I'm Malik, that's Dion, and she is Zira," he laughed.

Now I was lost. I was confused and couldn't explain why my children had grown so quickly and had died with me. I wasn't sure if we had another war with the Siberian Tigers or if something more heinous happened. My heart was racing like I had run a marathon and my heart dropped deep into my stomach. I was finding it hard to breathe because the guilt was plaguing my existence. How did I become so weak?

"I'm sorry," I cried to them. I tried to pull them all into my arms and shower them with hugs and kisses. "I'm so very sorry."

"But we're not dead, Mommy," Zira spoke. Wait a minute…Zira spoke with her mouth and not through telepathy.   What   in   the   hell   is   going   on?

I tried to gather my senses. I looked around the vast lands and tried to make sense of where I was and why I was there. But still, nothing came to me. If I wasn't dead, why was I here? Although I couldn't answer that question, I was sure that my little monsters could.

I released them from my motherly grasp and turned to Zira. The first thing I wanted to know is why is it I could hear her soft, angelic voice here but not at home. "I hear your voice," I told her.

She smiled at me and swung her body from side to side. "I can't hurt the dead here," she stated.

"If we were home, Zira's spoken word would wreak havoc on everyone around her," the lighter boy said to me.

"And which one are you? Dion?" I asked. I had tears falling rapidly down my face. Not because I was sad, but happy. I was seeing them in the future, and they were beautiful…all of them.

"Yeah. His ugly butt is Dion," the darker boy answered. As I analyzed them both, I could see Gethambe in them. The long, black, bone-straight hair should have been my first clue, but I missed it. The last time I laid my eyes on my three babies, they were only three years of age. Their sentences weren't even complete.

We all sat down in the grassy field. I had so many questions that I wanted to ask them before I was doomed to leave this paradise oasis. They sat down beside me and watched the sun with me as it began to descend behind the snow-capped mountain that was calling for me to climb it.

"Tell me about your powers so that I can better understand you guys."

"With one spoken word, I can cause the earth to quake. The Almighty showed me my power and said that one day I will know when to use it. He also said that one day I will be able to talk without hurting people. He said that my brother is going to show us how to use and understand the power of three," Zira explained.

"The power of three?" I questioned.

"Yes. Zira's power feeds from our energy," Malik answered.

"We give her power and protection and she gives us life. We are all equal but all weak. If one of us is missing, the unity is broken, and our power ceases to exist. We will become mortal," Dion said.

"So, you are fated to be together forever?"

"No. Once Lance arrives and becomes an adult, he will teach us how to live our lives separate but remain the power of three," Malik answered.

"And who is Lance?"

"Lance is the son you carry inside of you. He will grow to become Alexandria's defender. He will be the Achilles of Alexandria. He is Daddy Bullet's son," Zira explained.

"I will only have one?"

"Yes. Lance will be blessed as a demi-god but tasked with defending a mortal realm. He would never know what it would be like to morph into a lion or wolf. Like us, we will never know how it feels to will our beast. That trait is suppressed by our demi-god blood," Dion whispered, as if he was depressed about not having shape-shifting abilities.

"The war that we will fight will involve angels and demons. Fighting the Dark Lord and his new Queen of the Damned is on our horizon," Zira said.

"Dark Lords and the Queen of the

Damned…my…my…my."

"Mommy. You won't be able to fight in this war," Zira said to me.

"Why?" I questioned. "Am I going to die giving birth or something?"

"No. The war will begin on the night of the blood moon. And on that day, the last of your demi-god powers will be transferred to your last born – Lance," Malik explained.

"Haven't you notice that your powers have weakened?" Dion asked.

"Yes. But I thought it was only because I was pregnant. It happened before when I was pregnant with you guys," I replied.

"No. When we were born, you gave us a part of you. Although we didn't get your lion or wolf ability, we inherited most of your godly powers. You did what you were tasked to do. You brought together the two tribes. Now, all you have to do is help Serenity rule over Alexandria until we are grown," Zira said.

With tears swelling in my eyes, I asked, "Will I lose my lion and wolf too?"

"No. They will always be a part of you. But in order for you and our father to rule as equals, you have to become equals," Malik stated.

"We have told you more than what we intended, now we need to get you up that mountain so that you can wake up and we can guide you home," Dion announced.

"As much as I would love to climb that mountain, I feel like I'm a little underdressed for the occasion," I laughed, pointing at my naked body with both of my index fingers.

Zira looked at me, wiggled her nose, and immediately, I was fully dressed from head to toe in winter gear, and so were they. That let me know that I wasn't going to climb up that mountain alone, especially without my powers.

I stood up and extended one of my arms for my daughter to take my hand, and the other one for one of my sons to grasp. With Malik leading the way, all three of us started our journey toward that mysterious mountain that continuously called my name.

As we walked across the bluegrass field filled with dandelions, scenes from my life flashed across the sky. I noticed that every moment that flashed before me, was a moment that I shared with Bullet. Seeing those life events filled my heart with sorrow. Especially the scene that replayed the events that led up to the day he died.

I looked up one time and saw my mother and my father as they looked down from the Heavens onto us. My mother looked at peace and my father displayed a smile of approval. It warmed my heart to know that I had finally exceeded his expectations.

As we got closer to the mountain, I felt as if a weight had been lifted from my chest and I was able to breathe. The worries of my life had miraculously evaporated into the land around us.

"We're here, Mommy," Zira announced.

It seemed like we had just started walking and the mountain was so far away. But I was now standing at its base. But what was more mind boggling was, at the base of the mountain there were stairs. As I looked up, I noticed that these stairs swirled around the mountain, leading to the top.

"I never got the chance to ask you. Where is here?"

"Valhalla. The Heaven for the Almighty's most worthy warriors," Dion answered.

"This is Daddy Bullet's final resting place," Malik stated, pointing to the staircase.

Slowly, I took one step forward. Then another one. Then another one. Then another one until I was standing on the first step. When I looked down, what was once a stone block was now a golden step. As I stepped up to the next stone block, it too turned gold.

I turned and looked at my children and wondered why they were not following me. Hearing my thoughts, Zira answered, "This is a journey that you must make alone. When you see what is meant for you to see, come back to us and we will help guide you home."

I nodded my head and began my epic journey up the mountain. At first, my pace was slow because my heart became heavier with each step. But as Bullet's scent engulfed my being, my slow pace became a quick sprint. When I looked up into the sky and saw the flashes of our life together, my quick sprint became a full marathon. I was running rapidly up the steps as if I was running for my life.

Time stood still for me as I made it to the top of the mountain. I was freezing, my heart was hurting, and my body was tired. I looked forward and noticed that on top of this mountain, there was a whole village. As I started to walk, doors opened, and warriors stepped outside and pointed in the direction that I needed to walk. To my surprise, there were just as many women in Valhalla as there were men.

When I reached the small cabin at the end of the golden path, I noticed that its door had not opened automatically. As I stood facing the door, I became short of breath, my heart was racing, and my limbs became limp. Everything in my body told me to turn and run away. It warned me that I wasn't ready to face what lie waiting for me behind that door. But knowing that he was there gave me the courage to turn the knob and open it.

As it opened, there he stood by the fireplace, poking at the lumber that crackled as it burned. Nothing about him had changed. He was still tall, dark, and handsome. He still had that beautiful smile that pulled me into his essence. He was still the Bullet I had laid to rest.

He put the poker down and walked over to me. He was so graceful, so masculine, and so incredibly gorgeous. I couldn't stop my tears from falling as my eyes followed him across the room.

Bullet made it to the door, grabbed me by my hand and pulled me in to him. He wrapped his arms around my body, and I busted out into a full heart-breaking cry. Feeling his body holding mine reminded me that I would never have this man in my life again…not even in death because he would always reside in Valhalla.

"No, no, no, Mon Cheri. There is no need for the tears," he said, kissing me on my forehead and pulling me into his small cabin.

"Why did you leave me? Was I not a good wife?"

"I never left you, My Love. I am watching over you, the kids, and even Gethambe every day," he answered, sitting down on the floor in front of the fireplace and pulling me down onto the bear rug with him.

"Why didn't you wait? We could still be together. You could watch your son grow," I cried.

"Because, at that time, we didn't know that Serenity was strong enough to take on the Siberian Tigers. I needed our victory to be assured," he answered, running his finger down my cheek.

"But we had a plan. We were going to retrieve our daughter and we were going to bring her home…together," I told him.

"With all your visions, the threat on our family, and the crap that Lana was pulling, I needed to be sure that no one, outside of our people, could enter the gates of Alexandria. It is now protected with old magic and can only be broken by the Almighty himself. So, please Mon Cheri, don't hate me for loving you enough that I sacrificed my life," he pleaded, leaning in to give me a soft and passionate kiss.

"I miss you so much. And our son will never get to meet his true father."

"Lance," he smiled. "He will know about me and all that I have done for him and our people. He will know that I loved his mother with every breath in my body. And he will know that he was created out of love. Lance will know me through you, through Gethambe, through Serenity, through Malik, Zira, and Dion. And on his eighteenth birthday, when he's given his strength, he will make this same journey to talk with me. It will be then that he will realize that he has known me all his life."

"So, you already know his name?"

"Zira named him. The kids come here often. They tell me how bad my death has hurt you."

"Because I love you."

"It's okay to love me, Mon Cheri. But you have to let me go. Free my spirit so that I may enjoy Valhalla. I promise that we will be together again."

"Valhalla is for warriors."

"I'm only here until we are united. We will spend eternity in Edom. But you have to let go of all the pain of death and embrace all the memories of our life together. It is only then that you will find happiness. I need you to have your mind right and be strong for these kids. Serenity is a great big sister, but they need their mother," he said; his voice was filled with love and compassion.

"I love you, Bullet."

"And I will always love you. In life and in death, I will always love you, Mon Cheri."

He stood up and motioned for me to stand with him. Bullet pulled me into his arms and walked with me down the path that led to the stairs. As we walked through the small village, the warriors stood outside their doors with their swords drawn, making an arch for us to walk under. From the skies fell Star Gazer lilies, my favorite flower.

He walked with me down the steps until we reached the bottom. Before I grabbed Zira's hand, Bullet pulled me into him for another passionate kiss. I was smothered by his love for me, his gentle heart, and his passion for his family.

"Before you go, place all your trust in Serenity. She is going to have to decide between the man she loves and the deity she needs. Know that her final decision with be made out of love for her family."

"Does this small bit of information have anything to do with the upcoming war between the Heavens and Hell?" I questioned.

"No. This bit of information is for the decision she is going to have to make between Rouge and Maahes."

"Maahes? Who is that?"

"A powerful god who can either lead our people into a glorious victory or a dominating defeat. Everything is going to rest on Serenity's decision," Bullet answered.

"And what decision is that?" I asked.

"One that can change the fate of our people. You will understand what I'm saying more when that time arrives for her to make a choice. Just know that sometimes you have to let go of that old life to be blessed with an everlasting one," he smiled. "No more questions Mon Cheri. We did good raising her. Serenity loves her family and would sacrifice the world to keep them safe," he said. Bullet pulled me into him for a final kiss and then faded away.

Although I knew that I wouldn't see him again until I crossed into the afterlife, I had made peace with his sweet departure into Valhalla. Just knowing that he was still watching over us gave me the closure I needed to move on with my life. I wasn't letting go of him because I didn't love him anymore. No, I was letting him go because I loved him with all my heart.

I grabbed my kids' hands and as a family, we left the man I loved in a world of peace…Valhalla.

~~~~~~~~~~~~~~~~~~~~

Chapter Seven

Gethambe

Ashley had woken from her long slumber and immediately went into labor. In between her contractions she was able to tell me about seeing Bullet and finding peace. She also told me that after she gives birth to his son, she will become powerless. Her son will draw her powers into his being and grow to become Protector of Alexandria.

While Lilith and Na'amah worked hard to deliver our son into this ratchet world, Samael shimmered into view and asked that I join him for a walk. I knew that meant he wanted to talk with me without my wife listening in.

We made our rounds around the city and gathered up Rouge and Pax. Without warning of his intentions, Samael shimmered us all into the conference room in Achaemenid. That's when I realized that whatever he needed to say, we needed to listen to every word and take it seriously.

"Please. Take a seat," Samael said.

"What type of trouble is heading this way?" Rouge asked.

"As you know, Lana was denied entrance into Heaven.

She was sentenced to a life of servitude in Hell," he began.

I looked at Samael with disgust because I knew he was about to tell me something that was going to make my blood boil. He had been holding a secret and now that we were finding out more information about our past and the battles of our future, whatever he did, he had to come clean.

"So, she's in Hell," Rouge chuckled. "I don't think anyone here would be heartbroken about that."

"I am," Pax said softly. "I can't help but to still love my little girl." I looked over to see the tears swelling in his eyes. We had all forgotten how much he cared for Lana. She was his pride and joy…Daddy's little girl.

"I'm sorry, Father," Rouge apologized. "I'm sorry for being inconsiderate of your heart. But my sister and your daughter has turned her back on her people and denounced her own child. She's not the same Lana. She is damaged goods."

"I understand," Pax said; his voice was filled with sorrow.

"When her soul descended to Hell, I gave her to Lilith as a gift," Samael explained. He held his head high as if he was free from the evil deed that he was about to reveal.

"Get to the point already," Pax huffed.

"Somehow, someway, her biological father slithered his way into her life and earned her trust. He then went to the Dark Lord and gave him her hand in marriage. They will be wed tonight."

"And what does that have to do with me?" I questioned.

"Everything. It has everything to do with you, Gethambe. This unity is going to affect your wife, your home, and most definitely – Serenity," Samael responded.

"If I'm correct, by her becoming the wife of Lucifer, she will gain his powers?" Pax asked.

"Not all of them, but enough to wreak havoc on this realm. Once they are united and The Dark Lord gives Lana a third of his heart, she is going to come for Ashley and Serenity. This is the war I see," Samael explained.

"I will protect Serenity with my life!" Rouge yelled as he jumped up from his seat and slammed his fist down onto the table.

"I'm afraid that your life won't be enough," Samael confessed.

"What needs to be done? Serenity is working with Eisheth Zenunim to learn a protection spell while she goes on a spiritual journey," I told Samael.

His skin turned white as snow and his eyes illuminated an eerie grey glow. The conference room lights dimmed as a hologram appeared in the middle of the table. Samael has had visions before in front of us, but he has never allowed us to see them.

Rouge sat down in his seat and watched as clips of Samael's vision played like an old black and white movie. We all saw glimpses of Lana in her black wedding dress – and I must admit, she looked amazing. Death and Hell seemed to have done her some justice. We watched as her father and mother pleaded with her to rage war against our people. We saw as she sat with her husband in their chariot as their demonic army attacked Achaemenid and easily killed a mass number of Canine soldiers. And we watched as they summoned their demonic witches and warlocks to remove the spell that protected Alexandria. His vision ended with the death of Ashley and my children; and the powerful Serenity was on her knees as The Mad King was ciphering her powers using what I found out to be the philosopher's stone.

"What the fuck?" I asked. I had never been afraid of anything. But I never loved anyone as much as I loved Ashley and my children. Knowing that there was a possibility that they would die, shattered my heart. "I am Gethambe! I am blessed by the Almighty and gifted with the ability to protect those that I love."

"The future is subject to change depending on the choices made," he announced. "Believe that Serenity is going to be your savior, because your existence depends on her heart," Samael advised us.

"Always a fucking riddle with you! Speak clear English for once! What in the hell does that mean?" Rouge asked. Pax knew that his son had become upset by seeing Samael's vision which showed the fall of Serenity. So, to give him a little comfort, he placed his hand over his son's and assured him that Samael's visions weren't always set in stone.

"Rouge, you are going to make a great king. I can see that Alexandria will flourish under your rule. And Serenity will give you many sons," Samael smiled as he looked at Rouge.

"Rouge and Serenity will marry? She will accept him as her husband?" I asked.

"Yes. He will be the king of Alexandria," Samael confirmed. Then he turned his attention to me and said, "In his death, he will gain life. One that is much different from the one that he is currently living."

"Wait a fucking minute!" Pax yelled. "My son is going to die if he weds Serenity?"

"He will die. Whether it be for Serenity or the love of his people; Rouge will forfeit his life."

"Then how is he going to become this great king?" I asked. I realize that sometimes you must ask direct questions in order to obtain a specific answer.

"Because young king, he will be reborn, like the Phoenix. Out of the ashes there will rise a noble king. He will be king like no one has ever seen within these realms. His wisdom and appetite for equality will win you this war. And his love for your daughter will enslave him to Alexandria."

"Can't you just say exactly what you mean? Must you always beat around the bush?" I huffed. Even when I think I'm outsmarting him, he finds a way to confuse me.

"I'm okay with being reborn," Rouge said. "I will do whatever it takes to keep our people and the woman I love safe."

"That's good to know," Samael replied. "It's going to take you to help her understand that it is okay for her to take your life. Doing so, you can be reborn into the deity that will alleviate the demonic entities that will come for her."

"Serenity is going to kill me?" Rouge asked.

"With the Blade of Courage," Samael informed him.

However, before we could finish discussing the great battle, one of my Canine Crew members came dashing through the door. He had large gashes in his body and blood was spilling from him like a waterfall.

As we sprang to our feet and ran to his side, I caught his body before it hit the floor. Looking deep into his eyes, I saw fear. This was an emotion I wasn't used to seeing. At least not from any of my loyal soldiers.

"My Lord. We tried to fight them, but they were too strong. We didn't lose many, but we lost more than I could count. I'm sorry. I have failed you."

With his apology, he died in my arms. I then looked

at Samael who looked as if he had seen a ghost. I knew that he had some sort of idea of what took the life from my loyal soldier.

"Speak now demon-god or I will smite you down to Hell where you belong!" I grunted. My blood was scorching, and my beast was starting to emerge. It wanted me to sink my teeth deep into his throat and drank his blood.

"Aamon," he answered simply.

My claws were now extending to their full length and my canines began to protrude as the fury raged inside of my being. I needed something or someone to rip to pieces and my sights were set on Samael.

"What is an Aamon?" Rouge asked. He slowly began to back away from me. He knew that I was ready to pounce, and he was giving me ample room to declare war on this god of mischief.

"He's our counterpart," Pax answered. "Samael has nothing to do with this attack. The Aamon was sent here to gather information about your army by someone with great power in the Underworld. I've seen them before. Long ago, when the first war was raged, Maahes created our people and his brother, Lucifer created the Aamon. They were made in our likeness in hopes that we would be fooled, and they would take control of the upper realms. These creatures feed from extracting our fears of dying."

"Calm down, Gethambe. I mean you no harm and I didn't bring anything up from Hell with me," Samael explained. "This is the work of Abrey or The Dark Lord himself," Samael said as he too backed away from me.

"Then take me to them. I want to see these creatures with my own eyes," I grunted. "I fear no man or beast!"

"As you wish," Samael said. Then he waved his hands and we were all shimmered to a place unbeknownst to me.

"Is this Hell?" Rouge questioned; looking out of a window.

"And my home," Samael answered. "Welcome."

"What type of ape-shit trickery is this?" I asked, still half transformed. Hell was supposed to be a place where souls burned eternally. But looking out the window, my eyes were greeted by a desert paradise. Not to mention the home in which Samael lived…it was a luxurious mansion. It was a duplicate of the Taj Mahal except the inside was decorated with modern Arabian furniture and expensive art.

"Hell does have its advantages if you're one of its elite. I am privileged to these amenities because I am an angel who is married to a few of Hell's top demons," he smiled.

"Fuck all of that, where do we find these – Aamons?" I wanted to know.

"First, you must promise me that you won't shift into your beast. You are not supposed to be here, and this could cause me more problems than I need. Secondly, when I say that it's time to go…it's time to go. I don't have the time or patience for your bad boy asstitude, Gethambe. Save your energy for the battle that is to come. Raging war on their grounds will be foolish of you. Lastly, rules here are different than your glorified Achaemenid. So, if by chance you feel the need to rescue the damsel in distress…. DON'T!" Samael enforced.

"I'll keep him under control," Pax promised.

Samael looked a bit concerned about taking us on a tour of his secondary homeland. But I'm sure that he knew that if he didn't, I would make good on my threat. Although I couldn't actually smite him down to the depths of Hell, I'm sure that my darling daughter Serenity could.

As we left his home, I was amazed that we were getting into a limousine to take a tour of the Underworld. This place was no different than the upper realms. The only difference I noticed was it was extremely hot, and you didn't see the demons just walking around enjoying their life there.

The further we drove away from Samael's home, the more distressed the land became. I felt as if he was taking us to the other side of the tracks because the scenery became dreary. The land was dead, and the homes were made of thin tin and wood planks. You could feel the thickness of sorrow and pain in the air. Not to mention there was a strong aroma of funky armpits and rotten flesh that nauseated you.

Slowly, the car came to a stop in front of some sort of commercial building. Samael looked at us with uncertainty, then opened the door and proceeded to get out. Before taking any steps toward the building, he issued another warning to me. "Things here are much different than what you are used to. No matter what you see, DO NOT ENGAGE THE ENEMY!"

"And I told you that I got him," Pax re-enforced.

As we made our way into the compound and to the arena, I saw our doppelgangers. They were human with the ability to morph into wolves; the only difference was, they had a tail like that of a serpent. Samael hid us in a corner where we were able to see them, but they could not see us so easily. We watched as they practiced among themselves, but some were more violent than the others. I was shocked to learn that they fought to the death and those who survived were chosen for battle. I was sickened knowing that they had so little respect for life; for their family.

"Is this meant to be a joke?" Rouge whispered. "So, they're efficient killers but they lack discipline, unity, and order."

"That is what makes them so dangerous. They have nothing to lose but everything to gain. When they win battles, their status is elevated, and they are able to leave these forsaken lands. So, they fight to the death for a decent life here in Hell," Samael explained.

As I continued to look on, I could feel my rage igniting. Their leader was holding a young girl hostage and was offering her as a reward for the last Aamon standing.

Simultaneously, those wild animals began attacking each other. They mindlessly ripped apart their battle brother for a chance to win the young girl.

"What is so special about the human?" I wanted to know.

"Whomever wins gets to have her for dinner," Samael answered.

"Dinner as if they are going out to eat or she is going to be eaten?" Rouge asked.

"She will be devoured," Samael replied.

"We have to save her," I said.

"This is not our business and it is not your place, Gethambe. We are only here to observe, not start a war before we are ready to fight one," Pax reminded me.

"That is the circle of life here. To the Dark Lord, they are nothing more than wild animals. And the humans that are fed to them are worthless souls. Life here is valued by what you bring to the table. There's no equality or unity. And because they want to be in the inner circle so that they can be accepted, they will do whatever is required of them. See, you train your people out of the respect for life, young king. Here, they train for survival. And that makes them a little more dangerous than your precious Canine Crew."

"So what. They're still no match for us," I huffed.

"The difference between you and them is, their leader can summon hundreds of thousands of Aamon. You only have who you have," Samael stated as we continued to watch them fight each other like rabid dogs.

"I've seen enough," Pax interrupted. "This is a place I don't ever want to come back to. We need to get back to the compound and prepare ourselves for the battle to come."

"Excellent timing. Bullet's son is making his grand entrance. It is important for Gethambe to be there to support his wife. Once her son arrives into this world, soon after, Ashley will lose her secondary powers."

Within seconds, I was sitting on the bed beside my wife. She had just begun to push him out. Samael could have held me a couple of seconds longer instead of allowing me to witness my wife's sweetness opening wide enough for a child to come out of it. Hell, after seeing the baby's head pop out made me realize that I'm not packing enough to satisfy her needs.

With every push, her skin illuminated a serene gold tone as she gave birth to our son. Ashley had been waiting for a long time to see the child that she had created with Bullet. I knew that this child would bring her happiness; more happiness than my children had given her. But I wasn't upset by it. This child was her connection to a man that she loved and respected; a man that she was no longer able to share her life with.

"It's a boy," Lilith announced as she cut the umbilical cord and handed him to his mother.

I could see the love in her eyes as she looked into his. "Lance," she whispered. "I'm your mommy."

Ashley pulled him up to her breast and inserted it into his mouth. As Lance began to feed, the golden glow that illuminated her body during his birth, slowly began to dim. We all watched as her powers dwindled from her body and fueled his.

"My Love," Ashley said as she looked at me with a beautiful, angelic smile.

"He's perfect," I told her. "He took all my good looks," I laughed.

"Babe. I feel so weak," she explained; nearly dropping Lance from her arms.

I leaned over and grabbed our son as Ashley's eyes began to close. I looked at Lilith as my heart started to race with uncertainty. "Do something!" I yelled at her.

"There is nothing that I can do," she replied. "As soon as she pushed Lance from her womb and fed him; he consumed most of her powers. Ashley is changing, Gethambe. She's not human but she isn't an enchantress anymore."

"What am I?" Ashley murmured.

"A skinwalker," Agrat bat Mahlat answered as she shimmered into the room and stood beside Samael.

"A what?" I questioned.

"A human that can take the form of an animal – like you," Lilith intervened.

I held Lance close to my chest and gave him a kiss on the top of his head. It was then that I realized that I was holding a mortal and wondered how he would fit into a mythical world. I feared that his blood would excite the packs…maybe so much so that they would attack him for it.

"No need to worry about that," Na'amah said. "He will be protected for the next eighteen years. That's why he drained Ashley of her powers. No harm shall come to him."

"Are we certain of that?" I asked, placing my newborn son in the bed beside his sleeping mother.

"Yes," Agrat bat Mahlat answered. "He is destined to become a great warrior and protector of Alexandria. Lance will also lead the armies in Jericho, the city that will be ruled by Zion, Malik, and Zira."

"And what is to come of my wife?" I asked.

"She will reign as queen of Achaemenid, with you at her side. Don't think that she is weak because she does not have the powers of a god. Ashley's beast will keep her well protected – both of them," Agrat bat Mahlat advised me. "Unlike you, her essence holds three entities, her human, her wolf, and her lion. So, she is still a powerhouse."

~~~~~~~~~~~~~~~~~~~

Chapter Eight

Serenity

Before going to the Hogan, Rouge pulled me into a room off the main chamber and closed the door behind us. He pushed me up against the wall and buried his head into the crease of my neck. Feeling his tongue as it slid across its length sent a tsunami of shivers racing throughout my body. Every nerve was excited with want and my heart pounded in lust. His body pressed gently against mine making my inner voice scream out in want.

"Marry me," he whispered.

"You really want me with all the baggage of enemies I carry?" I asked, leaning my head backwards onto the stone wall and enjoying his soft kisses and seductive sucking.

"Yes," he growled. "Marry me. Marry me today," he pleaded.

I pushed him back and looked in his eyes and fell victim to his love. I could see that he truly wanted me and I'm sure he knew how much I craved him. But I had to be honest about his scent.

"Rouge, I need to tell you something. I am totally and

completely in love with you. You are everything I want in a man and a whole lot more," I said, referring to his manhood. "But, when we are this close and you are suffocating me with your feelings, I am pushed away by your scent."

"Please don't. I love you. I want you. Dammit Serenity, I fucking need you," he pleaded.

"I'm not saying that I'm not going to marry you. I'm just saying that this is the problem that my father had with my biological mother. Therefore, it didn't work between them," I tried to explain.

"That's not true, My Sweets. Before all hell broke loose, your father had made peace with their differences and vowed to love her as much as he loved Ashley," he told me.

"But what if I'm not as strong as my father? Will you wait for me? Will you continue to love me with this same energy even if I am unable to satisfy you sexually?"

"Even if you cannot hold your breath long enough for me to feel your sweetness hug my manhood, I would still love you. I don't define my heart by my hardness," Rouge vowed.

I pulled him close to me and smothered him with a snowstorm of kisses. I hate that our scent pulls us to our mate and when it's off, it pushes us away from the one we love. It is a flaw within our species that I wish the Almighty could change.

"Rouge. I will marry you." For the first time in my life, I witnessed tears swell in his eyes and stream down his face.

"Marry me today. Marry me right now, Serenity."

As much as I would love to marry him right now, I couldn't. We had people waiting on us so that I can take this spiritual journey. "After I complete the task that has been placed before me, I promise to run back to your arms and become your wife."

"Why wait? I want to share my last name and my life with you. Just in case something happens, like war starts right as you return, I want to know that we go into battle as husband and wife."

"But it won't be official until we consummate our marriage. So, it doesn't matter if we do it now or later. And to be honest, My Heart, I'd rather it be later. I'm a little nervous about having my first sexual encounter in front of a bunch of old demon-gods and my parents. And thinking about becoming intimate with you scares me."

"Why? Do you not find me suitable?" he questioned.

"Of course, I do. I'm scared because I am inexperienced and unsure if I can handle or please you," I confessed. "I don't know what to do and I've never seen it be done before."

"I have all the experience you need. I will teach you," he smiled.

I hit him on his chest and began to pout. I was a little upset that he has experienced sex with another woman. I should have been his first like he was going to be mine. "Who is she?"

"We are taught by human girls when we reach puberty. They give it to us in every position imaginable and in any opening we desire. Then there have been several chambermaids, but none that mean anything to me."

"And you really told me?"

"Because I will never lie to you or keep a secret. And if it bothers you that I fucked a couple of the chambermaids, I will move here to Alexandria with you where I haven't fucked anyone."

"You will do that for me?"

"I love you. I don't know when Cupid shot me with his arrow, but I am completely and totally in love with you, Serenity."

"Have you told my father?"

"We have his blessings. Now tell me that you will marry me right now."

"Yes. But only if you agree to marry me in my mother's bedroom. She is on bedrest and I couldn't marry you if she wasn't there."

"I would marry you standing in the middle of Hell while fighting the Dark Lord's demonic army."

I threw my arms around his neck and hopped into his arms. As he held me up, I looked down into his greyish-green eyes and planted a soft and passionate kiss onto his lips. Being with him made me feel complete; however, I cannot deny that his scent pushes me away…far away.

When he lowered me to the floor, we made our way to my parent's chambers. When we told them of our plans, my parents were excited but when Pax arrived, he seemed a little distant. I wasn't sure if it was me or if he was stressed about the upcoming spirit journey; but whatever it was, he was killing my vibe.

My father sent for the priest as Lilith and her sister-wives stepped in to help me get ready. My mother was holding Lance in her arms and crying as they helped me get dressed for my special day. Although she wouldn't say it, this is not how she wanted me to get married. I know that she envisioned the huge church, white roses scattered on the floor, an elegant white gown, and my father walking me down the aisle giving me away to Rouge. But I was happy just knowing that she was here to witness my union to the man I loved.

"Where did the time go?" she asked. "Where is my baby?"

"Don't worry Mommy. I'm always going to be your baby," I smiled at her.

"I just wish things could be different. I wish we had more time to give you the wedding you deserve."

"As long as you're here with my father and siblings, I'm happy."

"Oh. I almost forgot. Daddy Bullet said congratulations on your wedding. He will be watching from

Valhalla as you take your next step into womanhood."

I couldn't contain myself. I was jumping up and down in excitement knowing that my idol would be watching me from the warrior's Heaven. Like my mother, Bullet was the father every little girl wished they had. He was protective, funny, caring, encouraging, and believed in the unity of family. I've learned a lot from him and loved him just as much as I loved Gethambe.

Seeing me act so childish made my mother laugh. Even with everything that she has endured and all the obstacles that she had to overcome, my mother still found the energy to smile. She doesn't know it but being a part of her has brought me peace. She didn't have to accept or care for me, but she did. Ashley gave me all the love a mother could give her daughter.

When Lilith finished perfecting my innocence for my wedding, she snapped her fingers and I was instantly dressed in a gorgeous, vintage, lace wedding gown. I didn't want a veil, which made Lilith a little upset. When everything was in place, the same priest that married my parents arrived to perform the ceremony for me.

He walked in and bowed to Gethambe, then Rouge, Pax, and lastly me. He then said a prayer to the Almighty as Rouge and I stood there holding hands. My eyes were locked on his and his eyes were locked on mine. Because we weren't in Achaemenid, we didn't have access to the Well of Elohim, but the priest made sure to bring some of the holy water with him in a small bottle. He poured it into the Golden Goblet of Life and said another quick prayer over it.

He handed the goblet to Rouge first, since he was to become my protector and my king. Once he sipped from the goblet, Rouge gave it back to the priest who held it up to the Heaven's and said, "Protect this union, Lord Almighty. Grant them a long life of happiness and health. Let no man or beast break the bond that they will form this night."

Then the priest handed me the goblet and I drank the sweet, blessed water. When I returned it to him, he held the goblet high to the Heavens again and said, "Bless this child with many fertile seeds and sons for her husband.

"No markings?" I heard my father say.

"That is not the tradition here. Maybe when she returns to Achaemenid," the priest answered quietly.

Rouge looked at me and stated his vows. "Serenity, I promise my heart to you. There will never be another because the Almighty has created you just for me. I live to see you smile and I would rather die than to break your heart. You will be more than my wife. You are my better half, my equal and my soulmate. I vow to be with you forever, in life and in death. I love you."

With tears swelling in my eyes, I looked at Rouge and stated my vows to him. "Rouge, I promise my heart to you. There will never be another because the Almighty has created you just for me. Although I have power, your love is my weakness. I am powerless without you standing at my side. Together we are one, and we are strong. I promise to not only be the wife you desire, but the wife you need. I will be submissive, supportive, and bear you many children to carry out your legacy. I give my heart to you – forever and always."

"With the blessing of the Almighty and the support of the elders, I pronounce you husband and wife. You may kiss your bride. But remember, this marriage isn't valid unless you consummate the marriage in front of your friends and family before or during the next blood moon."

Rouge pulled me to him and wrapped his arms around my waist. I locked my arms around his neck, and we shared an intimate, passionate kiss. It may have lasted a little longer than usual, but because we had hidden our affection from everyone for so long, it felt good to show our love to the world.

When we parted and faced our loved ones as a married couple, I could see the acceptance in everyone's face except for Pax's. I don't know why he wasn't happy that his son had just became a king. I was giving my empire to them. By him being my chosen mate, he inherited everything.

As Rouge received hugs from my family and our friends, I made my way over to my new father-in-law. Trying to pull some sort of reaction from him, I extended my arms for a hug. Reluctantly, he turned his back to me and walked away. Unable to control my temper, I yelled out to him. "What is your problem, Pax?"

"You! You are my fucking problem!" he responded. Hearing our voices elevating on such a romantic evening, the room grew quiet.

"This isn't the time, Father," Rouge said.

"You must have lost your mother fucking mind. Who

in the fuck do you think you are talking to my daughter like that and in that tone?" my father inquired. His body swelled and became as hard as stone.

"No disrespect, My Lord…" Pax started.

"Father. What is it?" Rouge asked with concern plaguing his voice.

"Does Serenity know that she is going to have to take your life in order to save her people? Did you tell her that she is your Helen of Troy?" Pax spat.

"What is he talking about?" I asked my new husband.

He walked over to me and tried to pull me into him for a hug. "Samael had a vision that you will dagger me in order to win this battle. But we all know that his vision is subject to change."

"And you didn't think this was something I should have been told? What happened to no secrets?"

"Honestly, I was so happy that you agreed to marry me that it just slipped my mind."

"Serenity, I've known Rouge all my life. I believe him," my father added.

"Baby let's face that issue when we get there," my

mother said.

"But I'm going to kill the only man I love. What a wedding gift," I huffed.

Feeling awkward about Samael's vision, I needed some space. So, I left everyone in my mothers' room and bolted out of the door and down the temple steps. I needed some time to digest that I was going to take the life of my supposed soulmate.

When I came to my senses and stopped running, I was at the botanical gardens. Funny, this is the one place that gave my mother peace when she couldn't be with my father. So, I opened the door and walked inside to see if I could find my peace there as well.

There was a bench in the middle of the butterfly exhibit, so I sat there and allowed my heart to shatter into a million pieces. Nothing in my life has gone as it should. I was tossed away by my biological mother, estranged from my biological father for quite some time, desired by the Siberian Tigers, and now told that I have to kill my husband. *What's next?* I thought.

"You take my life and I will be reborn into a better

version of myself," Rouge answered, walking up to me.

"You should have told me. I wouldn't have married you and we wouldn't have to worry about this."

"Well, per Samael's vision, I'm going to have to forfeit my life regardless. He said I will either lay it down for you or for my people. I'd rather it be you since I love you so much more," he joked.

"Why? Why are you chosen to die? I feel like I'm cursed. Doomed to live this life as nothing more than a power source; unable to experience love or happiness."

"Nah. I'm going to make you happy and I have already showed you what love feels like," he smiled, kissing me on my cheek.

"You just want to have sex with a goddess," I joked.

"Nope. I don't want to have sex with a goddess, I want to make love to one. And I will. Right after this so-called spirit journey you're going to take," he said, standing up and holding out his hand for me to stand with him.

"Thank you," I said to him.

"Don't thank me until after I split you in half," he laughed.

"Whatever. It can't hurt that bad."

"For you, it can. But for me, it will be *AMAZING*!"

We laughed about it for a few seconds longer before making our way out of the building. As I held his arm and walked back to the temple, I wiggled my nose and changed our clothes. We needed to be in something a little less formal for my spiritual journey.

Before we made it back to the temple, we were met by my father, Pax, Juice, Stewart, and Joker. They redirected us and we headed toward the gates of Alexandria. The plan was, Pax would go on the spiritual journey with me, accompanied by Rouge. My father would be on the inside of the Hogan watching Nola as she guided me. He wanted to ensure that she wouldn't try to persuade my spirit to go elsewhere. And the outside would be protected by Juice, Stewart, and Joker...just in case my spell fails for any reason. But I was assured by Eisheth Zenunim that the magic that was taught to me was old magic and that the protection spell could only be broken by the Almighty. But the demon-goddess has been wrong before.

As the gates opened, I could feel the evil that

surrounded us. We hurried out in hopes that nothing slipped in. Although my mother was protected inside of the temple along with all my siblings, I was still worried about her. She didn't have her enchantress powers and if captured by the enemy, my father would surely give them whatever they wanted for her safe return.

We walked swiftly for about a mile where the small Hogan was located. Before getting to the entrance of the small igloo style hut, a woman appeared. She was tall, slender, with smooth cinnamon skin, and the prettiest turquoise eyes. Her clothing barely covered her thin frame and when I noticed how her beauty captivated every man around me, I became paranoid.

"Welcome, Serenity. It is a pleasure to meet you," Nola said with a soft and innocent smile.

I didn't acknowledge her. Instead, I pulled out my staurolite and labradorite stones from my pocket and placed them on the ground, circling the Hogan. On the outer side of the crystals, I made a second circle using blessed salt from the Almighty. When the circle was completely closed and everyone inside of it, I started my protection spell.

Nola didn't see it coming when I pulled her to me and slit the palm of her hand. She yelled out in excoriating pain as I pulled her around the Hogan and allowed her blood to fall to the ground. With every drop that spilled from her hand, smoke came up from the ground.

When I completed the circle for the third time, I invoked my spell of protection:

This circle is our power of protection,

To keep us safe from the evil intentions.

This is our shield from the demons that wait,

To take our light and blessings away.

With this shield, no evil shall prevail,

Let your will be done and send them back to hell.

Upon my last word, the ground beneath our feet shook violently and a ring of fire surrounded us. As I looked at Nola, I saw nothing less than respect. She knew that I had been trained in magic that was older and more rooted than hers.

"Eisheth Zenunim?" Nola questioned.

"Does it matter?" I snapped. "Let's get on with it."

She bowed her head in defeat and welcomed us into her home. We left Juice, Joker, and Stewart outside to keep a watchful eye on our surroundings just in case something popped off. As we entered her domain, I did a spiritual protection spell over myself, my husband, and my father-in-law so that Nola couldn't tamper with our spirits as we walked through the Valley of the Shadow of Death. Lastly, I kissed my father and cast a protection spell over him, keeping Nola from entering his mind and toying with his reality.

"Eisheth Zenunim must really trust you to teach you so many old spells," Nola smiled wickedly.

"Actually, she doesn't like me at all. She just wants to fuck my father," I answered her sarcastically.

"What a naughty little mouth you have. Your parents should have taught you better manners. Oh, my apologies my queen, you don't have a mother. How rude of me," Nola clapped back. "Didn't your mother disown you? Now she is about to reign supreme as the Goddess of the Underworld," she laughed, taking a seat in front of the fire.

"No. My mother loves me. From the day I slid from my ratchet carrier till today, my mother has, and always will, love me."

"Kudos, Serenity," she smiled mischievously. "I

respect that you accept Ashley as your mother. There needs to be more women like her and less women like our true kin."

The men couldn't understand my hostility towards Nola, because she had been nothing but kind as far as they were concerned. But I knew who she really was, because her demon presented itself to me. Nola was a succubus that pulled men into her essence with her hypnotizing voice and exotic looks. Once she had them under her spell, she would sex them to death while feeding on their essence.

We took our seats in front of the fire and waited for Nola to begin the ceremony. She said a chant in her native tongue and then reached into the fire and pulled out some golden dust. She held it in the palm of her hand as she blew it softly into our faces.

As I inhaled the golden mist that swirled around my body, I was flooded with a cluster of mixed emotions. At first, I was pissed the fuck off as I rekindled my childhood. It didn't matter that Ashley took me in and treated me like her own; I hated Lana for not even giving us a chance. That bitch deserved to die a million deaths and her soul should cease to exist. But the more I thought about her the more I accepted the fact that we would never accept the other for who they were. Then, I couldn't stop laughing. I was overwhelmed with joy. Memories of Bullet raced through my mind like a Nascar. The glimpses were fast and poetic; showing me his heart and how much he truly loved me. When I arrived at the memory of his funeral, I felt at peace and at one with my surroundings. I was enveloped in tranquility.

"Walk by faith," I heard a voice tell me.

I opened my eyes and looked around. As I glanced at my new reality, I noticed that I was standing on a cloud, looking down onto the earth. I focused my eyes so that I could see my surroundings clearly. I could see demons climbing on top of each other, making a pyramid to come and get me. I also noticed that many of them were meeting their demise as Pax and Rouge fault heroically.

"Ask, and you shall receive," the heavenly voice said.

With my heart pounding violently against my chest, I decided to take a step forward and follow my heart. I felt that my protectors were efficient at handling all the demonic entities that would love to capture my spirit and offer it to Lana. So, I followed my heart and walked slowly into the peaceful light that was pulling at my soul.

As my body was immersed in love, I could feel the weight of doom and stress be lifted from my body. I knew then that I was in the presence of greatness.

"My soul is tormented and needs a resurrection; guide me," I pleaded, dropping to my knees.

"Rise and I shall show you the way," he said. The sound of his voice showered me with acceptance and forgiveness.

I stood to my feet and looked into the bright, serene light and saw my destiny play out in front of me. I was shown how to enter the tomb beneath the great temple, where to find Pandora's box, and how to use the Blade of Courage to sacrifice Rouge in order to release Maahes.

"This can only be done by a descendant of Sheba who is unsullied," he said his voice was soft and pure.

"Although I am married, I am still a virgin," I confessed. Not because I wanted to be, but we hadn't had the time to become as one and unite our spirits.

"Once the sacrifice is made, things will be as they should be. Rouge will be reborn into a king worthy of your heart," he said; then I felt a tap on my heart, and I fell backwards onto the earth.

When I opened my eyes, my father had his sword drawn on Nola. It angled in a way that if she had moved an inch, her jugular would have been sliced. I looked over to see Pax and Rouge who had just begun to stand up. There bodies were covered in blood and they had many slashes from the battle they fought to keep my demons at bay. But something was different about how I saw Rouge. I still loved him with all my heart, but my spirit was now craving the love of a beast. What did the Almighty do to me?

"We need to go," I demanded.

"Where to, Babe?" Rouge questioned.

"Back to Alexandria so that I can fulfill my destiny. I realize what I have to do and why."

"What is that?" my father asked.

"Sacrifice my heart to release the beast. Maahes is the key to our survival and it's my innocence that will control his beast."

~~~~~~~~~~~~~~~~~

Chapter Nine

Lana

My dress was specifically made to fit my body. It was made of the finest lace and satin with small diamonds embellished into a swirly design. My hair was braided loosely from one side to the other; allowing a long ponytail to hang freely. The braid itself was intertwined with a string with small diamonds, giving my hair an eye-capturing shimmer. Lei was kind enough to do my make-up. She was a sweet and gentle soul, but I knew that I needed to keep my eyes on her. I could see small hints of jealousy dance around her aura because she thought it should have been her that he chose. She had been his concubine for decades, and I could tell that Lei harbored deep feelings for Lucifer. It slipped out in her actions and the words that she chose to tell me about him.

"I'm not taking him from you," I whispered; placing my hand on top of hers.

"He's going to love you in a way that he could never love me," she answered.

I was breaking this woman's heart the very way that Ashley broke mine. I was taking someone that she loved and cherished, someone that she had spent many years with, someone that she wanted to marry and carry his child. Although I felt like shit for doing so, I couldn't turn back. I wanted this; I wanted him and all the power that he would give to me.

I smiled at her and replied, "He is going to love us equally. We will share his heart."

When she looked into my eyes, I could see the newfound respect that she had for me; for my kindness. "No jealousy?" she asked.

"None whatsoever," I smiled. "He's both of ours," I said. I meant that from the bottom of my heart. I didn't care if Lucifer fucked her brains out nightly. I was going to be the one wearing the ring and carrying his son. Lei would be nothing more than my bitch. A fine ass bitch at that.

She leaned in and kissed me softly on my lips. The feeling of her lips touching mine sent small tingles racing throughout my body. For a brief minute or two, I wanted a little more than a kiss from her.

"I am yours to do as you please. Whenever you please. I pledge my body to you and your husband," she murmured, giving me a more intimate kiss.

I allowed her to seduce me with her flirtatious ways, but I refused to allow her to go any further than giving me a passionate kiss. Although she was pledging herself to me, I knew that this was a dog eat dog environment. My heart told me that Lei would throw me under the bus and take my crown if she could. However, I wasn't as dumb as she would have liked me to be.

Pulling away from my new sister-wife, I looked at myself in the mirror and marveled at the masterpiece she had created. I stood up and ran my hands down the contour of my body as I twirled around. After about three or four spins, I stopped and admired how elegant I looked. I was perfect; from the top of my head to the bottom of my feet, I was perfect.

As I continued to look at myself in the mirror, I noticed a shimmering shadow in the corner of my bathroom. When I turned around to get a clear view of what it was, my heart sank deep into my stomach.

"Lilith," I hissed.

Her body slowly emerged from the darkness and she

was accompanied by her sister-wives. Lei saw her and immediately stood up and bowed to her out of respect. Lilith didn't even acknowledge her presence; her gaze was fixed on me.

"You clean up well, dumb queen," she said, smiling wickedly at me.

"Wish I could say the same about you," I snapped.

She laughed slightly and moved closer to where I was standing. She extended her arm and placed her slender finger over my lips. "Ssshhh," she whispered. "You don't want to piss me off."

I pulled my body away from her and waved my hand, motioning for Lei to leave me with the demon goddess. She looked at me and then at Lilith. I could tell that she was hesitant to leave me with them alone.

"I will be okay," I told her.

"GO!" Lilith yelled. Within seconds, Lei was running out of the door. She moved so fast that the wind from her body made the door slam harshly behind her.

"What do you want, Lilith?"

"Nothing," she smiled.

"Then why are you here?"

"To see if the rumors were true. To see if the Dark Lord really dug to the bottom of the barrel to find a bride," she chuckled.

"Yes, demon-bitch. I am about to marry the King of the Underworld and become your queen. You will bow to me and do my bidding," I said; returning the same evil smile she had greeted me with earlier.

"I would never bow to you, dumb queen. And neither will any of my sister-wives. Although you will become the Queen of the Damn, I still out rank you. So, I guess you will still be bowing to me and doing my biddings," Lilith laughed hysterically.

"That's impossible!"

"Ask the Devil himself. You will never be our superior or our equal. I not only have the blood of a demon, but I was the first woman created with the blood of the Almighty. Read your history, bitch, or learn from *"an old hoe"* like me," Lilith snapped. I could see her eyes darken and her temperament change.

How could this even be possible? I was going to marry

the Lord of the Underworld and gain a portion of his powers. How is it that Lilith would still reign supreme over me? Before I had a chance to dig deeper into Lilith's story, Lucifer walked in the door. Needless to say, he was escorted by Lei. Although I appreciate her concern, now I know I really need to watch her sneaky ass.

"Is there a problem her ladies?" he asked

"No," Lilith grinned.

"We only dropped in to congratulate Lana on her upcoming wedding," Na'amah said; her face was emotionless.

"Well, you said your congratulations, now get the fuck out of our home," Lucifer huffed. I looked over to see as his body swelled and his muscles became well-defined. He heightened my emotions when he used his hand to throw his long dreads backwards. I believed I had inadvertently climaxed by watching him flex his power.

"As you wish, My Lord," Lilith said, bowing her head.

"Oh, and by the way," Lucifer laughed. "If I catch you around my wife or home again, I'm going to pull your soul from your body and confine it to a genie lamp. And while your body lay dead in my dungeon, I'm going to allow the foulest demons to fuck you in the ass while you watch from that tiny space that you will call home."

"No need for that, My Lord," Samael said as he shimmered into view. "I will make sure that my wives stay far away from Lana and your residence."

"Make sure you do," Lucifer snapped. He waved them away and then focused his attention on me.

"Lilith hates me because of Ashley. She stopped by to inform me that I would never be as powerful as her or her sister-wives."

He walked over to me and wrapped his arms around my waist. He pulled me close to him and smothered me with passionate kisses. "Don't let Lilith get to you. She's a little upset that its not her that I am marrying."

"So, is it true? Will she remain more powerful than me after we become one?" I questioned.

"It's true," Lucifer answered. "She was created by the Almighty and although she was shunned from his graces, she is still favored by him," he answered. "But as long as you remain faithful and true to me, you will have nothing to worry about."

I couldn't help but to smile flirtatiously at my soon-to-be husband. But I would be lying if I said I wasn't jealous knowing that Lilith's power would still trump mine. Even after I would gain a third of the Dark Lord's. It made me feel that there was just no beating this bitch.

"We have a wedding to attend," he smiled, wrapping his arm around mine.

"We do," I agreed.

With the moon high in the sky, together we walked into the Garden of Death and Destruction. The garden was filled with Lucifer's top ranked soldiers and elder demons. Although it was a little warmer than I would have liked, the scenery was gorgeous. We were surrounded by red and black roses, accented with Baby's Breath. It was slightly foggy and there was a faint scent of rosemary mixed with jasmine which gave me a sense of euphoria.

As we approached the sacrificial alter, I saw Cherish and Abrey. However, this time I wasn't mad or upset, I was engulfed in serenity.

Lucifer escorted me up the steps where I noticed two young women wearing black sheer robes. I looked at my husband in confusion because I was at a total loss of what it was that I was supposed to do.

"To become the queen of the Underworld, you have to commit the ultimate sin. Together we must take the lives of these young virgins and suck the blood from their hearts," Lucifer informed me.

"They barely look eighteen. They are just babies," I replied as my voice trembled.

"These Hellions are a thousand years old. Once they reach their eighteenth year, they stop aging. Hellions are bred once every five thousand years. They are the product of the union of my son and daughter."

"Your son and daughter mated?" I asked in disbelief. Then I heard a noise coming from behind me. I turned around slightly to see my father approaching us with a silver box in his hands. When he reached the alter, he stood in front of us and opened the box. There were two small silver daggers on each side of a large golden one that lay snuggled in the middle. My eyes immediately locked onto the large golden dagger. On its handle there were three large stones; a ruby at the tip, a sapphire at its base and a beautiful blood diamond in the middle.

"Let me tell you a story," Lucifer said as he picked up one of the smaller daggers and motioned for me to grab the other one. "When I fell from the Heavens and my wings were clipped, the Underworld opened up. For a long time, I was here alone, so from my blood I created Asmodeus and Astaroth. Although they were brother and sister, Asmodeus seduced Astaroth and produced many children. The purest of our bloodline were twins we call them, Hellions."

"And what about our son that you will impregnate me with tonight? Will he too marry one of your female seeds?" I asked; my stomach was now turning knowing that it was expected for brothers and sisters to fornicate.

"It is our tradition here for each brother to marry his sister. He will marry the daughter that I had created with Lei. Together they will rule the western boarder of the Underworld," he grinned. Lucifer then motioned for the two Hellions to come to us. As they walked in our direction, they disrobed.

Lucifer looked at his descendant and used his finger to make an X on her chest. As he etched it into her body, that

176

same X appeared on her twin brother. Out of nowhere, a demonic entity appeared and pushed them down onto their knees. As he pulled their spirit from their body's, we plunged the daggers deep into their chest. With surgical precision, we cut out their hearts and began to drink the blood from them.

When their body's fell to the ground, they caught fire and disintegrated into ashes. After draining their hearts of all their contents, I dropped my Hellion's heart onto the ground. My euphoric feeling that overwhelmed me in the beginning wore off and I began to feel as if I was intoxicated. I instantly became drowsy, my surroundings were spinning out of control, and I could feel as my heart slowed.

The chanting became loud and my beautiful dress was laying on the ground, sliced into a million pieces. My mother and father helped me to the altar and my father lifted me on to it. Cherish pulled my arms up above my head while my father parted my legs.

I wanted to ask what was going on, but I couldn't move, and no words would form. I looked up to see a blinding white light and then to the right of me to see Lucifer holding the golden dagger. He was totally nude and regardless of all the shit I had going on around me, all I could do was focus on his large dick that hung past his knee. Not only had his manhood increased in size, but he had morphed into his demon form.

He stood at least ten feet tall, he had two large horns protruding from his head, and as I looked downward, I noticed that he had a tail and hooves for feet. But what surprised me the most was his large, black wings. As he flexed his body, they flared out and I noticed that his feathers had hints of ivory that shimmered under the moon.

I don't know how long I was out for, but when I woke, I found it hard to breathe and I was laying in my bed. I looked down to see what was causing the pain in my chest and saw a scar on the left where my heart was located. As I tried to readjust myself in the bed, I felt wetness beneath me. I was able to throw the comforter back and was shocked at the amount of blood I was laying in.

"What happened?" I said aloud.

"You were quite tight," I heard Lucifer say. "We had to cut you a little for all of me to squeeze inside of you."

"What? You cut open my vagina?"

"Just a little," he laughed. "My demon dick is a lot bigger than my human one," he explained.

"Am I with baby?"

Lucifer walked over to the bed and kneeled beside it. He reached over and grabbed my hand and said, "Not only do you hold a piece of my heart inside of you, but you are also pregnant with our son."

"And what type of demon am I?" I questioned. I was hoping like hell that I wouldn't be some dreadful, soul eater.

"You are an enchanted vampirina."

"So, I'm not a soul eater, I'm a blood sucker? Wow."

"You're so much more than that. You may crave the blood of a human, but your real power lies in your sorceress. I have a library filled with books of spells and hexes and in time, you just might be as powerful as Eisheth Zenunim," Lucifer said, toying with my emotions. "Now let's get you cleaned up because your new kingdom awaits you." Then he kissed my hand and helped me out of the bed.

We made our way into the bathroom where the chamber girls had drawn my bath. Lucifer undressed himself and pulled me into the warm water with him. He pulled me close to him as I wrapped my arms around his neck. It was then that I heard his heartbeat thumping against his chest. I tried to ignore it and just enjoy being held by him.

I laid my head in the crease of his neck and noticed that his jugular vein was vibrating. I could hear my stomach growling with want, I began to feel nauseated, and my head started to bang as if I was recovering from a hangover. Although Lucifer was talking to me, I didn't hear a word he said.

I used my tongue to lick the very spot I was about to bite, then, without warning, my canines extended, and I had implanted them deep into Lucifer's neck. UHM, his blood was so sweet and divine. To my surprise, he didn't try to push me away, instead, my husband allowed me to get my fill.

"That's right Baby, take me," he moaned softly. When I couldn't drink anymore, I released his neck and began to shower him with kisses.

Lucifer pushed me backwards and asked me to float on my back. I did as he wished and waited patiently for him to take my body. He cupped my ass and pulled my body close to him. He parted my legs and dipped his head between my thighs. While cupping my ass, he gently licked and sucked on my lady. As I relaxed my body, and bathed in the pleasure of my husband's tongue, small waves of desire paraded inside of me.

When he finished, he pulled me over to the edge where we stepped down into the water and took a seat. I watched him as he stroked his hardness passionately, observing how the veins protruded from its shaft. I licked my lips, slid between his legs, and inserted him deep down my esophagus, but even then, not all of him could fit into my mouth. Slowly I bobbed my head up and down its length as I tightened my grip and twisted my hand on it seductively. I made sure to look at him while I pleasured my master, it excited me to see him biting on his bottom lip in satisfaction.

With my other hand, I gently massaged his balls as he ran his fingers through my hair. At times, when he enjoyed me the most, he would grab a fist full of my hair and thrust his hips upward while shoving my head downwards.

"Shit! Lana dammit," he growled. "Take it all down your throat."

But I had other plans. I wanted to feel the beast inside

of me. I pulled back and then re-examined my situation. Lucifer had an extremely large package and he told me that they had to cut me open slightly for him to fit it inside of me. So, I looked at him and waited for him to give me some direction.

"You will be okay," he said in a low voice.

So, I hovered my body over his and slowly descended onto it. Inch by inch, I eased down his hardness. I could feel as he stretched me to my limits and still tried to gain more space. When he was fully submerged into my wetness, I wrapped my legs around his body and slowly began to swirl my hips.

He grabbed one of my breasts and inserted it into his mouth while caressing the other one. He became excited quicker than I anticipated. I could feel him growing inside of me as the veins in his shaft pulsated viciously. He was moaning loudly as he began to thrust up into me.

My body was shivering in desire and I could feel my cream warm. I began to bounce on him at a moderate speed, taking every inch of his manhood deep into my sweetness. As our bodies slammed against each other in an erotic dance, the water splashed wildly around us.

"Slow down, Lana," he begged. "You're going to make me cum."

"Shut up nigga and fuck me!" I yelled. My body had been deprived of love for so long that I was fighting for this climax. "Fuck me hard!"

"You want it hard, Bitch?" he growled.

"Yes! Yes! Yes, Daddy!" I screamed. My lady was tingling, and I was on the brink of a massive explosion. I had a hurricane of sexual tension building up and banging on the door to be released. Every touch from him was intensified. I was drunk off his Grey Vetiver cologne and seduced by his moans.

Lucifer pulled out of my sweetness and tossed my body over the rim and slammed deep into me. He was pounding violently in my sweet spot to an erratic tempo. He pulled me back by my hair as I tried to crawl away. Then he held me in place by my hip as he called me every dirty whore he could think of.

"Don't you dare run from this dick. You wanted it and as your husband, Bitch, I'm going to give it to you!" he roared.

The strength of his voice shook the walls and made the chamber girls run for cover.

As my blood boiled in desire and I yelled out in satisfaction, I felt my body surrender to its new master. I soared high into the heavens and climaxed on a cloud of luxury.

Lucifer now had his nails deep into my thighs as he continued to power drive swiftly. I could hear him breathing loudly, I could feel drops of his sweat slide gracefully down my ass, and he was yelling in ecstasy.

With the last thrust of his hips, he erupted inside of my cavern. His grip tightened and his body stiffened as his cum forcefully shot out of him and into me. I felt as his manhood jerked and throbbed inside of my body as it poured out like lava. I backed my ass up and rolled my hips as his body slowly came to an earth-shattering halt.

I was exhausted and didn't have the energy to lift my body from the tub. This had been a very intriguing twenty-four hours and a memory that I would cherish forever.

Lucifer pulled out of me and carried my weary body over to the shower. Like a good husband, he lathered the sponge and washed my body. He signaled for the chamber girls to help me out when he was finished and ordered them to dress me in something enticing for the evening.

"Something angelic," he told them. "Showcase all of her assets for every demon in the Underworld to see. I like seeing others lust for what they can't have."

"Oh. I'm sorry about feeding from you. I couldn't control it, My Lord."

"I prefer that you only feed from me or one of your chambermaids. I'm a jealous man and don't believe in sharing. So, never dishonor me by feeding from another man, demon or human."

"Yes, My Lord."

The ladies escorted me to my dressing room and began to tend to my needs. As they scurried about to get me dressed, my father slithered his way into my quarters.

"I'm so proud of you," Abrey said.

"Really?" I asked sarcastically.

"You owe me for helping you to get where you are," he grinned.

"How much are you asking for?"

"Just a little assistance obtaining an ancient relic."

"Okay. And how do I go about helping you obtain such a relic?" I questioned.

"Your demon reared its ugly face last night revealing your vampire and sorceress. So, I need you to rifle through your husbands' old books and find out where the philosopher's stone is hidden and how to obtain it. I'm sure it is hidden by magic, which is something you now possess," he grinned mischievously.

"Tell me why you want this stone again."

"Because I can use it to cypher Serenity's powers from her body and place them into mine."

I turned to look at my father to see if he was pulling my leg. Why in the hell would I give him an ancient relic to take Serenity's powers when I could use it and cypher her powers for myself? After all, she was my daughter.

"So, let me get this straight. You want me to not only find it, but you want me to hand it over to you? Since I'm already a powerful being, wouldn't it make sense that I add her powers to mine?"

"Don't cross me on this child," he said angrily. "You

will lose everything you have and then some if you don't give me what I want. I'm sure that the Dark Lord has explained his jealous rages to you. He will not only dispose of the man who places a kiss on your lips and confesses his love for you, but he would dispose of you too. I have many men willing to die for me and my cause, so don't test my patience."

"Alright. I'll do it. But you must promise me that once you go to war and you're finished with Serenity, you will give her to me. Along with Ashley and every child she has bred into this world."

"Deal."

"Give me a couple of days."

"I need it before the next full blood moon."

"It will be done. Now go home to your pathetic wife and allow me a couple of hours of tranquility with my husband."

Abrey disappeared quicker than what he appeared. I continued to get dressed but my mind was racing a marathon. I thought about ways to trick my father into giving me Serenity's powers so that I could dispose of Gethambe and his entire family. Although I'm happy, I still harbor much hate for them in my heart.

~~~~~~~~~~~~~~~~~~~~

Chapter Ten

Ashley

I woke up this morning and felt like I was a prisoner in my own body. I was filled with hatred and rage; nauseated by the smell of innocence. I was on fire and I had a thirst for blood. I felt the need to cause death and destruction to this beautiful place I once shared with my husband, Bullet.

I could hear my son crying and I knew that he needed to be fed, but I had no will or want to feed him. Instead, I yelled for the wet nurse to come and take him away. I knew in my heart if I had allowed him to stay close to me, I would have snapped his neck.

I saw the three younger kids playing together quietly. It irritated me knowing that they were happy while I stood here suffering. How could they sit there and play blissfully when death was surrounding our very being? They may be children, but they knew what was going on around them. Little bastards.

I slid my body out of the bed and stretched. I looked over towards Zira who was now staring at me. Her eyes said everything they needed to say. That little deceitful monster didn't trust me. Zira didn't trust her own mother. Who in the fuck did she think she was?

I inched over close to where they sat, now grabbing the attention of all three kids. Before I could get close enough to snatch the very life from that ungrateful daughter of mine, the little monster shielded herself and her brothers from my grasp. Then she whispered to me telepathically, "*I don't want to hurt you. Leave us and we shall let you live.*"

Really? She views me as a threat? It's because of me that she is even blessed with her powers. How dare she say that to me. "I will save this fight for another day, young one," I said aloud.

I turned and began to walk out of the door when it slammed closed. I looked back at the red-haired demon with pure hatred in my eyes. Moving as one, she and her brothers stood up and began to analyze me. Zira's face was emotionless, her eyes were cold, and all their bodies glowed an eerie color of ivory. But they didn't scare me in the least; I was ready for them.

"Let her go," Malik said to me.

"Whatever are you talking about?" I questioned.

"We can see you," Dion responded.

"Of course you can see me. I'm standing right here," I told him.

"If you don't release our mother, we will expel you by force!" I heard Zira yell at me.

Now I was pissed. These little ingrates were challenging me. So, I pulled my hair up and wrapped it into a sloppy knot and braced myself for the impact.

Zira ran quickly towards me, jumped about three feet into the air, and slammed her small body against mine. The force of her blow sent me sailing backwards into the wall, shaking the temple as if the earth was quaking. *"Free my mother!"* she demanded.

It took me a second or two to shake off the pain that ran rampant in my body. But as I pulled myself together, repositioned my clothes, and kicked off my slippers; I was battle ready. I ran towards my daughter, with lightening speed, dropped to my knees and slid across the floor. When my body approached hers, I extended my fist and punched her in the gut. Zira's body bent forward, and she fell onto the floor. She lifted her head up and looked at me in surprise. But that wicked smile she displayed told me that she was about to kick my ass. Zira stood up slowly and shook her head a couple of times. Without saying a word, her brothers were standing strong slightly behind her. Now the fight begins.

This time when Zira came charging towards me, she was accompanied by her two brothers. Simultaneously, they leaped into the air and rained down a thousand blows to various parts of my body. Zira landed the last power punch onto my face, knocking me onto my knees. As I tried to defend myself and punch back, Malik caught my fist while Dion right and left hooked me in my midsection.

My body was sore, but my drive to win the battle was high. So, I focused all my energy and released a powerful explosion from my aura that sent them sailing across the room. Their bodies smashed into the walls, leaving large cracks. By this time the lionesses came running through the door to see what was going on. When they saw that the kids and I were in a heated battle, they too charged me.

With a snap of my fingers, they were immobilized. They looked like chess pieces on a chessboard. They could see and hear everything, but they couldn't move.

Malik was fully charged even after his devastating impact with the wall. Zira pointed at him and he morphed into his adult self. Dion ran to her side to help fuel her power. I tilted my head to one side and then the other, allowing it to crack several times, then motioned for him to bring the fight to me.

He ran up to me, grabbed me by the arm, swung my body around a couple of times then threw me into the wall. Before I could get up, he was sitting on top of me with his hands wrapped securely around my throat. Unbeknownst to me, this was only a distraction while the other two rug rats summoned the demon-goddess herself, Lilith.

"How dare you possess a descendant of mine," she huffed, tossing three stones onto the floor.

Malik released his grip from my neck and left me laying on the ground. As I tried to get up and charge after him, I found that I had been imprisoned. That evil whore had trapped me.

"It's me, Lilith. It's Ashley," I said politely.

"Don't toy with me, dumb Jinn. I can see your aura as it dwells inside of Ashley," she snapped.

By this time, Eisheth Zenunim shimmered into view and released the spell that I had placed on the pride. Zira and Dion returned Malik to his normal self, but they kept a watchful eye on me.

"Expel the demon from Ashley," Lilith ordered Eisheth Zenunim.

She gracefully walked toward my host and entered the triangle that held my essence hostage. She kneeled and began to draw ancient markings onto the floor with her fingernail as she chanted softly to herself. When she started her spell, I began to pace the floor. There was no need of me attacking Eisheth Zenunim because I knew I couldn't win against a witch as powerful as her. And even if it was possible for me to defeat her, I would still have to try and defeat Lilith and those three little brats that stood with her.

Eisheth Zenunim stood up and placed her hand on my chest. As it began to illuminate, I could feel it heat up and shake slightly as she whispered;

From the depths of Hell, you have risen,

Holding this body, you have imprisoned.

Stealing its light and controlling her soul,

Taking the place of what you don't own.

With evil intentions, you live and thrive,

Killing the aura that's locked inside.

Free her spirit, and leave her be,

To Hell you must go, immediately!

My heart began to race and the room around me became distorted. My body felt weak as I fell to my knees. Without warning, I began to vomit; throwing up the Jinn that took possession of my body while I slept.

I looked up to see Lilith and Eisheth Zenunim. I had never been so happy to see them. Lilith extended her hand and helped me up from the floor, as Eisheth Zenunim began to question the Jinn.

"Who sent you?" she wanted to know.

"Only he who can," he answered.

"Lucifer?" she asked.

"Eisheth Zenunim, you're smarter than that I hope," he chuckled.

"Abrey?" Lilith questioned.

He looked at her and smiled wickedly. "Perhaps."

"Why?" I wanted to know. "What have I done to him?

We have never met."

He laughed hysterically before answering, "Because you're the bitch that helped to create Serenity."

"Destroy him," Lilith ordered.

"Wait, wait, wait," he pleaded. "Let's make a deal."

Before Eisheth Zenunim could react, Lilith raised her hand to stop her. "What information could you possibly offer me?"

"Something that could enlighten you on your current situation," he answered slyly.

"Don't listen to him," I begged Lilith. "I was inside of his head when he inhibited my body. He is full of lies and deception."

He glared in my direction with hostile intent, but then smiled mischievously. "Then you will know if I'm lying."

"And what do you require in return?" Lilith asked.

"Once I give you this information, my very existence is doomed. All I ask in return is that I be released and Eisheth Zenunim cloak my aura."

"Deal," Lilith agreed.

She didn't listen to me and that pissed me the fuck off.

I stormed up to her and slapped her in the face. "How dare you make a deal with him after what he has done to me and my children!"

"Touch me like that again and I will forget who you are and beat you down like a runaway slave. It would be wise of you to take a seat on your bed while I handle this demonic entity," she said softly.

"Just you wait until Serenity arrives," I hissed. "She would not like the way you are treating her mother."

She paid no attention to me, only focusing her attention on the Jinn. Instead, she lifted her arm and pointed to the spot she wanted me to sit in. I reluctantly followed her directions without fussing with her.

"Now tell me what you know," she demanded.

"The Mad King is soliciting the help of the new Queen of the Damned so that he can find the philosopher's stone."

"And why should we care about a useless rock? I couldn't care less if he wants to change metal into gold," Lilith said sarcastically.

"It has another use," Eisheth Zenunim chimed in.

"It has another use," the Jinn grinned. "It could be

quite troublesome for a powerful deity such as….Serenity."

I gasped and was at a loss for words. After hearing him speak of a way to harm my baby, I panicked. Lilith could see how worried I had become but made no gesture to come over to me to help soothe my uneasiness. How was I to save her? Who was going to help me save my baby?

"What else could it be used for?" Lilith questioned.

The Jinn giggled uncontrollably as he spun himself around in circles. "A way for the Dark Prince of the Underworld to become a god," he hummed.

"He could use it to cypher Serenity's powers to achieve immortality. He would gain all her strengths and none of her weaknesses. He would be equal to Maahes," Eisheth Zenunim explained.

"That can't be possible. Maahes was created from the rib of Lucifer. They are brothers whose powers are nearly equal," Lilith stated. "Serenity's being doesn't hold that type of power."

"It's not only Serenity's power that he plans on taking," he chuckled.

"Lana's?" Lilith asked; her skin turned a pale white.

"What?" I yelled out. "How powerful is she?"

"Now do you get it?" the Jinn said as he danced around like a happy fairy. "I don't want to be found once The Mad King receives that kind of power."

"How do we stop him from getting that stone?"

"You can't," he laughed. "He has the Queen of the Damned in his pocket. She will hand it over to him blindly; not knowing that she has a target on her back too. Now cloak my being and free me. I gave you all the information you need to balance this war out."

"No he didn't!" I yelled.

He stopped laughing and looked at me with disgust. He knew exactly what I was referencing. He may have told us about Lana and her powers, the philosopher's stone and what Abrey intended to use it for, but he neglected to give us a remedy on how to defeat The Mad King.

"The only other piece of information that I could possibly offer you is, Maahes is the key to winning this war. He must be released, and he needs to accept Serenity as his soulmate. But, with her recent wedding, that might not be so easy," he grinned.

"And why is that?" Eisheth Zenunim questioned.

"Because her heart and body must be pure. If she has given herself to her new husband, he will rebuke the quest for their union," the Jinn explained. "Now that is all I know…free me," he demanded.

"As you wish," Eisheth Zenunim agreed. She then performed a cloaking spell to hide the Jinn from any demonic entity of the Underworld. When the Jinn thought that they would release him from the circle, Lilith stepped towards him with a genie lamp in her hand.

"What is that!" he yelled.

"The prison that someone created for me and your new home," Lilith smiled. "Once Eisheth Zenunim places you inside this lamp, I'm going to bury it deep beneath the ocean floor where no one would ever find you," Lilith smiled.

With Eisheth Zenunim chanting her spell to place the Jinn into the genie lamp, he rambled off a billion swears to them. I watched as his essence turned sky blue, money green, and diarrhea brown.

"Consider this as me being nice," Lilith advised him. "Instead of allowing you to exist, I should allow my sister-wife to devour your soul. How dare you to be bold enough to bring harm to my doorsteps and then try to bargain with me. You should have done more research about who I was and how I roll," she stated elegantly. Within seconds, his body was sucked into the lamp and the genie lamp was vanished.

With my nerves rattled, I yelled for the wet nurse to bring me Lance as I started to gather my children. I knew that I wasn't powerful enough to protect my babies from the demonic attack that was to come, but I also knew that there was no place that they would find us. Besides, I couldn't leave before Serenity returned with Gethambe. So, I sat back down on the bed with my children huddled around me and cried.

Agrat bat Mahlat, Na'amah, and Samael shimmered into my chambers. I'm sure they overheard what the Jinn had just revealed to Lilith. I didn't know if they came bearing more bad news or a remedy. I just know that I fell into a black hole of hopelessness and misery.

"As soon as your family returns, we will get you and the kids to safety," Lilith assured me.

"I need to be here, fighting alongside my husband and daughter," I said, choking on my words due to the steady stream of tears that poured from my eyes.

"Ashley, this is a battle that you can't fight. These kids need their mother, especially Lance," Na'amah said, as she wiped the tears from my eyes.

"My kids don't need me. They are all able to protect themselves. It's me that you're really worried about. Little old mortal me," I said with my voice trembling. It made me wish that the Jinn possessed my body again so that I could have some type of power.

"Man up and stop all that fucking crying. Your stupidity is beginning to remind me of another queen that I can barely stand to be near. So, what, you don't have your powers. Get over it already. You passed them down to a generation that is going to need them way more than you do now," Samael barked.

"What?"

"Your job was to unite the tribes and give rise to a demi-god. You did that and more. You raised Serenity, birthed the power of three, and gave life to the future Hercules. Your job now is to make sure they live long enough to fulfill their destinies. It's not about you anymore," Samael's words were precise and harsh.

"The Almighty has opened Seventh Heaven for you and the children. He is offering you protection during this war. He knows how special you and your kids are and refuses to allow any harm to come to any of you," Agrat bat Mahlat announced.

"What about Serenity, Gethambe, Rouge, the Canine Crew, the wolves, and the lions? Are they not special too?" I questioned.

"Some lives will be sacrificed for thousands of lives to be saved. This is the circle of life," Lilith said, trying to soothe my aching heart.

"Will I be able to see them before we leave?" I asked.

"Of course. You have to be here when your daughter is united with Maahes," Samael answered.

"So, he will accept her?"

"Serenity didn't have time to consummate her marriage to Rouge. When Maahes is released, he will be drawn to her and she will be drawn to him. They will share an everlasting love for each other. Serenity will ground his beast and Maahes will protect her with his life," Samael answered.

Hearing him speak in that reassuring voice eased all my uncertainties about our fate. I cannot deny that I hate knowing that I have to hide in Seventh Heaven with my babies as a war raged on over the lands I have come to know as home.

"They're back!" I heard one of the lionesses' yell. "Open the gates!"

I jumped up from my bed and handed Lance to Lilith as I ran to my husband. I was running as fast as my legs could move, pushing people out of my way to get to him. When I reached the gates that just began to open, I stopped and stood perfectly still. My heart was racing, sweat was pouring down my body, and I was trembling with anticipation. I couldn't wait to see him.

When the gates opened and I saw Gethambe, I ran to him and leaped into his arms. As he spun me around in circles, I showered him with passionate kisses.

"I wasn't gone that long," he joked.

"I love you so much," I confessed.

"I love you too," he laughed, lowering me to the ground with his muscular arms still wrapped firmly around my body.

I laid my head against his chest and glanced over at Serenity who was smiling at us. I whispered to her, "I love you."

"I love you too Mommy," she whispered back as she grabbed ahold of Rouge's arm and began to walk into the city.

"Come on Baby. It isn't safe out here," Gethambe said to me.

I laughed slightly as I reminisced about what had just happened inside of the city gates and said, "It's not safe in here either."

I was talking about the Jinn possessing my body but my husband's appetite for my wetness had him thinking about something else. He forgot that everyone could hear his naughtiness.

"Daddy," Serenity laughed.

"What?" he answered her with confusion.

"We can hear you," Rouge laughed.

"Yes. We surely can," Pax agreed.

I pulled my husband into the gates and watched as they closed behind us. As we made our way to the temple, I whispered to him that Samael and Lilith needed to speak with them before I could welcome him home properly.

"Fuuuuuccccccck!" Gethambe yelled. "I need some pussy!"

~~~~~~~~~~~~~~~~~~~~~~~

Chapter Eleven

Gethambe

Ashley had been stressed with all that has been happening, so I decided to take her on a small vacation. Lilith told me about a private beach on Paradise Island; home to the Amazons. I had decided to take her there and be back before the blood moon when Serenity is to release Maahes and the final war begins.

The island is cloaked from the human world as well as the Underworld. However, it took quite some time to convince her to go with me and leave our children behind. Ashley was concerned about their safety, even with Serenity, Lilith, Na'amah, Eisheth Zenunim, Agrat bat Mahlat, Pax, Rouge, the pride and the entire Canine Crew watching over them. There was so much power in Alexandria that even the Almighty had to be impressed.

Lilith had a private beach house located on Paradise Island that she willingly gave us access to. She was even nice enough to shimmer us there and notify the Amazon women of our arrival. They didn't mind much that Ashley was visiting, but with me being a male was a different situation. Men were not a being that they welcomed with open arms. But thanks to Lilith, they approved my stay for a couple of days with the exception that we had two guards with us anytime we were outside of the beach house. They wanted to make sure that I wouldn't wander about the oasis paradise they called home.

We arrived right before the sun began to set on the ocean. I had enough time to fix us a quick meal and pack it up for a beach picnic. I had to convince Ashley again that the children were fine in order to get her to go to the private beach and spend a little quality time with me.

We only had to walk a few steps to the shoreline, and I took the pleasure of spreading a blanket on the sand for my lovely wife to take a seat. We were just in time to watch the sun setting. The sky was decorated with the glorious colors of magenta, burnt orange, amber, with streaks of crimson. I sat down on the blanket with the basket beside me and then pulled my beautiful wife down to me.

Her mocha skin shimmered under the setting sun, her face was just as young and angelic as the first day I saw her, and her smile captivated my soul. She was everything a man could ever hope for in a woman.

She looked at me and smiled slightly and reminded me how much she loved me. I cupped her cheek and pulled her to me. I gazed into her alluring hazel eyes and became one with my soulmate. Then, I planted a soft and gentle kiss onto her lips. It started off as a simple peck that soon evolved into a tongue twisting battle between two lovers.

"Can we have a little privacy?" I asked the two gorgeous Amazon women who watched my every movement. I didn't mind giving them a show, but I did promise Lilith that I would mind my manners. Besides, they were a distraction that I did not need. I needed to focus all my attention on Ashley and making sure she was satisfied and relaxed.

"We were told to stay with you," the younger girl stated.

"But if you feel uneasy about showcasing your abilities, we would happily turn around to spare you the embarrassment," the older lady giggled.

I couldn't believe this prehistoric virgin was trying to call my bluff. She better be glad that Ashley wouldn't be willing to give me a threesome, or else I would blow her ancient ass back out. I would shove my dick so deep into her pussy that she would be giving me head backwards because the tip of my dick would be coming out of her damn mouth. And to make it even sweeter, I know all these bitches are virgins; I'm dream walking in a gentleman's Heaven.

"I was born to perform," I smiled with confidence. Then I focused my attention back onto my wife.

She was laughing at the young girls who she believed were flirting with me. Her giggle warmed my soul because it had been so long since I had actually heard her laughter. I leaned over to my wife and eased my body on top of hers. I held myself up on my elbows and blessed her face, neck, and breasts with intimate, soft kisses. As she lay beneath my body, I could hear her moan quietly and she swirled her hips seductively.

"I need you," I whispered softly into Ashley's ear. Teasingly, I nibbled on it.

"Then take me," she replied.

I slid her white, silk panties to the side and eased my hardness out of my shorts. Slowly, I pushed the tip of my hardness into her wetness. I instantly became excited with her warm, juicy, tightness that surrounded me with passionate love. I could have surrendered my nectar upon entrance, but I had to hold out to prove my point to the prying eyes who watched us with eagle eyes.

"Mmmmm, you feel so good," she moaned, rotating her hips slowly.

"Dammit, Ma, this shit ain't no joke. I miss making love to you," I growled, as my beast began to emerge.

I powerfully thrusted my hips and drove deep into her being. She wrapped her legs around my waist and pushed up onto my steel rod eagerly. Gracefully, I slid in and out of her wetness, savoring the exotic feeling that enraptured my soul.

I could feel my balls tighten and my breathing become heavy with desire. Her intense seduction of my emotion made my heart skip a beat with pure enthusiasm. I was perspiring desire and crying in love.

I looked down at my wife as my hardness thumped heedlessly inside of her. I noticed that her eyes were shut, and she was biting on her bottom lip fervently. She was breathing in short, quick breaths; panting like a thirsty kitten. I could feel her heartbeat quicken as her cavern became wet with her sweet cream.

"More," she begged; her voice was soft and harmonic.

Obliging her wishes, I pulled one of her legs up onto my shoulder and increased my slow stride into a modest tempo. I was now slamming my body vigorously against hers; digging deep into her soul.

Hearing the waves crash against the shore, smelling the ocean breeze mixed with her sweet scent that captivated me, and feeling her soft, wet body beneath mine made my body shiver with sincere yearning for her heated cream.

"I'm close," she confided in me. "Give it to me, Daddy. Please," she cried.

So, I acted as if she was a nail and I was the hammer. I pounded in her viciously, trying desperately to satisfy her needs and my desire to release. I pulled her other leg up onto my shoulders and pushed them back until her toes were digging in the sand. She instantly became my submissive and I her master. Her body was now under my control. Ashley squirmed, yelled, prayed, and cried as I dipped deep into her body.

My manhood was hard, and I became more and more excited each and every time that my beautiful wife tried to escape our sexual escapade. She knew better. As I chased the prey to my climax, my beast emerged, and I sank my teeth deep into her neck. My claws extended giving me the extra edge I needed to hold her in place.

I hammered inside of her until she exploded. She spilled a sea of cum as her body shook violently. The warm gush triggered my quest for gratification. So, I continued to pound in her until I fell off the Great Sphinx of Giza and into a luxurious cloud of euphoria.

As I shot my hot nectar into her small frame, my body bucked wildly, my heart raced, my blood heated to a scorching degree, and sweat poured from my body like a waterfall. Ashley was trying to catch her breath as mine became lost in excitement.

When our bodies came to a halt, I fell slowly down onto her. It had been so long that I was sure that we would be stuck together for hours. At least we had food nearby that could hold us over until my hardness decided to decrease enough to release me from heaven.

"Well, you do know what you're doing," the younger Amazonian said.

"At least she pretended like you did," the other one stated.

"I've been around the block once or twice and have gotten the hang of it. Let me know if you want to take it for a test ride," I teased. But that comment didn't go over well with the wife.

"Say that shit again and you will feel like you're serving a life sentence. Because it will be a cold day in Hell before I allow you to get some of this again," she said playfully.

"Shut up," I told her, showering her with kisses. "I don't do pussy punishment. Because what you won't do, a chambermaid would," I laughed.

We laid there and talked until I was able to pull out of my wife. When we were able to separate, we gathered our things and went back to the beach house where we showered and fell into a deep slumber.

Ashley and I only stayed two days because she was eager to return to Alexandria. She missed the children and worried about their safety constantly. So, to ease her mind, I cut the trip short and called for Lilith to take us home.

Upon arrival we were greeted by Serenity who was in the first day of her heat. She wanted desperately to mate with Rouge but knew that she had to wait until she released Maahes.

"I had to cast a spell to keep her locked in this room. Her hormones are driving every male mountain lion and wolf insane. They can smell her heat for miles," Eisheth Zenunim explained.

"And I have been trying to keep Rouge from kicking in the door to get to her. He had become mad with desire," Lilith stated.

"It's been a fucking circus around here and all the animals are acting out of character," Samael stressed. "Everybody wants to fuck, including me. Everybody is getting laid except for me and Rouge because my wives have to babysit, and Rouge isn't allowed to taste Serenity's sweet innocence."

"Well, tonight is the blood moon. So, we need to get Serenity to hold off for a few more hours. After she retrieves Pandora's box and release Maahes, she can mate and consummate her marriage to Rouge.

"Lucas needs to help us retrieve Pandora's box," Lilith announced, in a low voice. She knew that that name angered me.

"Why in the fuck do we need to invite that bitch to the party," I growled.

"Because he knows the old traditions and will be able to oversee the union between Serenity and Maahes," Agrat bat Mahlat stated.

"Trusting him is like trusting Lucifer. Serenity said he wants Maahes' powers for himself. How do we know he will do what is right?" I inquired.

"Because I will be watching," Samael answered. "I cannot perform the ceremony because I am not an ordained priest. But I have seen it done many times and will know if he is trying to be slick."

"You mean to tell me that Lucas is a priest?" I huffed.

"Unbelievably, yes," Samael confirmed.

"The world is really going to shit," I said, making everyone laugh. "Well, first thing is first. We need to gather up the kids and Ashley so that they can make their journey to Seventh Heaven."

"We will handle that," Samael advised. "Kiss your wife good-bye and then I need you and Pax to head to Achaemenid to retrieve Lucas."

I walked over to my wife and pulled her to me. I gave her a kiss and said, "Don't get comfortable up there. Your home is here with me. I'm nothing without you."

"I feel like a coward, Gethambe. While my family is fighting the biggest war in history, I will be hiding in Seventh Heaven," Ashley said to me.

"Don't you ever let me hear you say that shit. You're only going there because someone must take care of our children. I would go but I cannot breastfeed Lance," I joked.

I could feel that I eased her mind about leaving us to fight, but she still wasn't happy. "I'm going to miss you," she said.

"Don't be up there fucking with those damn angels either. I don't want to have to go to Hell for clipping one of those bitches' wings," I huffed.

"This is all you," she promised, giving me another kiss. Ashley grabbed the kids and walked over to Samael who shimmered my family to safety.

I turned to Pax and asked if he was ready. He nodded his head in agreement but suggested that we take Rouge along for the ride. Pax felt that he needed to put some distance between him and Serenity while she was in heat. So, I opened the Portal of Life and stepped in to the swirling ball of lights while pulling my best friend in with me.

As we reached Achaemenid, Rouge was able to focus. We walked back to the holding cells where we found Lucas in good spirits. He was sitting in a chair that was positioned in front of the fireplace, enjoying my Kentucky Bourbon.

When we entered the room, he didn't even look in our direction. He continued to gulp his dark liquor which pissed me the fuck off. This motherfucker was enjoying my home as if it was his. I'm going to have to have a chat with my wife about the accommodations that are provided for our prisoners. Jail isn't supposed to be luxurious.

"Let's go Lucas," I said. Although I tried to use my polite voice, my tone was still harsh.

"Where?" he asked.

"Does it really matter?" Rouge spoke up.

"Of course it does. A man would like to know if he is

going to meet his demise," Lucas answered. I could hear the smile in his voice.

"Today isn't your day to die," I informed him.

"Ohhhh," he said, laughing slightly. "Serenity is in heat and she needs me to help her free Maahes? I told her she would come begging for me to help her obtain Pandora's box. I guess she didn't want to grovel on her knees, so she sent her bitches to do it for her."

I couldn't help myself when I lunged towards Lucas, knocking the glass from his hands, and yanking him up from his seat by the neck. With one hand, I was choking the life from him. I didn't care if he was a priest and we needed him to help us. My desire to kill him outweighed my need for his help. I'm sure we could find someone else to do what needed to be done.

"Don't do it," Pax pleaded. "We need him, Gethambe."

If it wasn't for my family, I swear I would have put that pussy out of his misery. But I listened to Pax and tossed Lucas's body into the wall like a rag doll. I wanted him to get up and challenge me, to give me a reason to end him, but he didn't. Lucas stood up, wiped the blood from his mouth, and laughed.

"Where is that sexy little minx with the leaky pussy? She was a lot nicer than you, Gethambe," Lucas taunted.

"Bent over on her knees, waiting for her husband to come back home," I laughed.

"She's married?" he questioned.

"To me," Rouged teased. "That sweet, juicy, tight pussy is all mine."

"Then you need your Almighty to come down from the Heavens and save your people because Maahes will deny her union," Lucas laughed.

"Shut up and walk," Pax demanded. He then pulled Lucas by the collar of his shirt.

I opened another portal and we stepped inside and returned to Alexandria. As soon as we stepped into the city, Lucas knew that Serenity's virginity was still intact. Her scent made his eyes turn dark shades of green and a deep color of yellow. He wanted her just as bad as Rouge.

"Such a sweet and tantalizing aroma," he grinned.

"Take him away before I kill him," I ordered.

As they escorted him out of my presence, Lucas yelled for Serenity, begging her to choose him to be Maahes' host. "I would give you the world!" he yelled.

After removing him from my presence, I had to confine Rouge who was beating on the door to my chambers. Because I couldn't imagine putting him in a holding cell, I placed him in Bullet's old room and had Eisheth Zenunim place a sleeping spell on him. This way, I knew he wouldn't get ahold of Serenity, and if she so happened to escape my chambers, he wouldn't be able to perform. This shit was wearisome, and I needed a mental break.

I had the chambermaids bring me a couple of blankets and I slept in the throne room. It sat in between my chambers and Bullet's. We only had a couple of hours to go because the chamber that holds Pandora's box only opens during a certain time on the eve of the blood moon.

Personally, I can't wait until this shit is over. Serenity has everyone on edge, including me but not for the reason one may think. I'm on edge because I don't know what to expect once this Maahes character reveals himself and I can't imagine losing my best friend, Rouge.

You think Pax is hurting, look deep into my soul and you will see my heart breaking as well. Rouge and I have been close for years. I have never fought a battle without him at my side. He was not only my right-hand, but he was my brother. Maybe not by blood, but he was still my family. I trust Rouge with my life.

Now, I'm going to have to put my trust in a god we know nothing about. I have to allow my daughter to sacrifice her happiness to release the deity that is going to save us all. This is unfair and total bullshit.

But I will worry about all of this when I wake up. I pray that this all ends well and that everyone finds peace. I don't want to spend eternity fighting with the Underworld. I want to spend eternity laying pipe to my wife.

~~~~~~~~~~~~~~~~~~

Chapter Twelve

Serenity

The time had come for me to descend into the tomb beneath the Great Temple. I was uneasy about making this journey. I knew that once I opened Pandora's box, there would be no turning back. I would have to sacrifice Rouge's body so that Maahes could return.

During my spiritual journey, the Almighty showed me a glimpse into my future. He allowed me to see that although Maahes would inhabit Rouge's body, his spirit would live on. Maahes and Rouge will become one and our union will conquer the Underworld.

Also, the Almighty showed me a glimpse of Maahes' past life. He was in love with a woman who was given to Lucifer as a gift. This female became pregnant by Maahes and he petitioned the Almighty for her hand in marriage. Before he was able to rescue her from the depths of Hell, Lucifer caught wind and ripped her baby from her womb and impregnated her with his own demonic seed.

Maahes found out what his brother had done and became obsessed with revenge. No demon or tortured soul was safe from Maahes' murderous rage. Seeing that his soul had become darkened, Lucas betrayed him and helped trap his soul in the Blade of Courage. To keep him safe until a super-power was created, the Almighty placed the blade inside of Pandora's box and sealed the entrance with a purified portion of Lilith's blood.

Now that Lana is married to the Dark Lord, and the Dark Prince has their blessings to rage war upon our people, I'm tasked with releasing this monster in hopes that my soul bonds to his. Not only are we to mate, I need to become pregnant with his seed. It will be my heart and our child that will control the beast. I will become the replacement wife that he was promised so many decades ago.

As I sat on my mother's bed and tried to weigh my options, only one made sense. As much as I hate to give Maahes the body of the man I love, I have no choice. Without his allegiance, we cannot win this war. I hold enough power within me to fight, but with the threat of the philosopher's stone hovering over my head, the possibility of Lana and Lucifer joining into the battle, and the thousands of Aamon's they can create in a matter of minutes, I realize that our road to salvation begins with Maahes.

I heard a knock on the door and then it opened slightly. When I looked up, my father was easing his way into the room. He was accompanied by Pax, Juice, Stewart, and Joker – but not Rouge.

"It's time," he whispered.

"Where is my husband?" I asked with my heart filled with sorrow.

"We thought it would be best if he doesn't go on this journey," Pax answered.

"Shit. I don't know if I should go. Serenity has my dick hard as fuck," Stewart announced, as he desperately tried to reposition his pants.

But he wasn't the only one who was excited by my scent. He was just the only one who was bold enough to say something. My father was the only male in the room who wasn't affected by my heat. He was nose blind to it.

I stood up and started for the door. As I got closer to the males, the louder their moans became and the more my lady leaked in want. It was so hard to control the succubus bitch who was clawing at my spirit and begging me to mate.

She didn't care who it was with, she made my lady tingle with desire. The feeling was so intense that it was becoming hard for me to think clearly.

We stood behind the main throne chair and I recited an incantation to remove the protection spell that kept the tomb sealed for so many years. I used my nail to slice my palm and allowed my blood to spill onto the floor.

"What did you do that for?" my father asked.

"In order to open the tomb, pure blood from Lilith's bloodline has to be given as an offering," I explained. "It was her blood that sealed his fate and it has to be her blood to revive him."

The throne chair levitated into the air revealing a small wooden door. I used my power to move the chair and place it on the other side of the room. I then kneeled and pulled the door open. I looked around at my protection detail and waited for one of the male escorts to take the lead.

"Into the depths of Hell we go," Joker said as he took the initiative to go first.

I allowed Stewart and Juice to go before myself, leaving my father and Pax to bring up the rear. We had decided earlier that I would be in the middle of the men because we didn't know if I would have my powers or what type of trouble we may encounter. The Almighty didn't give me much insight into what all challenges I would have to face as we entered Maahes' tomb.

We traveled down into the darkness for about ten minutes. When we reached the landing, torches lit without me having to use my magic. As I looked around our surroundings, I noticed that all the males had morphed into their beast. When I tried to communicate with them, I couldn't; we had been disconnected.

"Follow the path," I heard a female say. "Leave them there and come to me." The voice in my head was extremely soft and inviting. I felt as if I knew the entity that was calling out to me, so I began to walk down the dimly lit path.

I could hear the men howling as if they were trying to warn me not to go, but something was pulling at my spirit and I had to follow my heart. When I looked back at them, it seemed as if they were stuck behind an invisible forcefield because none of them could enter the tunnel.

As I walked closer to the opening, I was pleasantly

surprised to see that that dingy tunnel led to an underground paradise. It was full of flowers, huge trees, a stream, and exquisite green grass. It was gorgeous and serene.

I saw a young lady sitting in the grass by the stream, so I approached her. When she turned and looked up to me, you could have knocked me over with a feather. I was staring into the eyes of Queen Sheba herself. There wasn't a word I could use to describe her immense beauty.

"Have a seat," she said. Her voice was soft and soothing.

"Thank you," I said, sitting down beside her.

"Doesn't that sound amazing?" Sheba asked.

"What?"

"The sound of the stream flowing, the soft melodies of the birds, and the leaves rustling on the trees. It's like music to my ears," she smiled; bumping against me gently.

I closed my eyes to try and focus on the sounds that gave her peace, but I couldn't hear anything. I could see that the stream was flowing, and the trees swaying; but I couldn't hear anything that had to do with nature.

"I don't hear anything," I admitted.

"Oh," she giggled. "That's because you are burdened with stress. Don't be. You're doing the right thing."

"How are you so sure?" I wanted to know; as I looked into her comforting grey eyes, admired her long black hair, and wished I had her sleek curvaceous body.

"Because Maahes is your twin flame, silly," she answered.

"My twin flame?" I questioned.

"A twin flame is deeper than your soulmate. It's like a carbon copy of yourself but created to awaken your spirit and challenge your being. He is going to bond with you spiritually, mentally, and emotionally in a way that Rouge could never understand," she explained.

"That's deep."

She then pointed to the stream where a small golden box had surfaced. As I retrieved it from the water, Sheba said, "Love him with every breath in your body and he will love you with every breath in his. He will give you the world and ask you for nothing except for you to love the man within the beast. He has been waiting for a long time for this moment."

"What about the woman he wanted to marry?"

"She was his soulmate during that time period, but not his eternal flame. It wasn't meant for their love to last beyond the birth of their child. Lei's heart belonged to the Dark Lord, from the day her soul had been sentenced to Hell. To her dismay, he didn't love her the way she desired."

"So, what really happened between them?" I questioned.

"When Lucifer refused to make Lei the Queen of the Damned, she tricked Maahes into getting her pregnant. She then told Lucifer that Maahes was petitioning for her release from Hell so that she could marry him and raise their child together," she explained.

"And I'm assuming this pissed off the Dark Lord?"

"Yes. But things didn't go as she planned. Lei figured that when she told Lucifer about her intimate relationship with Maahes and their unborn child, he would give her what she wanted," she said, as her voice lowered to almost a soft whisper.

"Is that when he killed Maahes's baby?"

"Lucifer may have pulled her unborn child from her womb, but it was because she begged him to. But what she didn't realize was her deceitful ways would cause a rift between her and the Dark Lord. She has blessed him with many children, but he doesn't acknowledge any of them as a true heir to his kingdom."

"Wow," I exhaled.

"Think of Lei as the serpent in the Garden of Eden, pitting brother against brother for her own personal gain. She not only lost the love of Maahes, but she became nothing more than a whore for Lucifer. She is of no threat to what you will build with the God of War and Protection."

"So, are you assuring me that Maahes will not go running back to his soulmate after I give him my husband's body?" I needed to know. I felt that if there was the slightest possibility of him doing so, there would be no way in hell that I would release his spirit.

"Rouge is your soulmate, but you cannot tolerate his scent. Maahes is your twin flame that is going to protect you with his life. With them combined, you will have the best of both worlds. You are not losing Rouge, he will still be there. His spirit will just become more enlightened."

"Will his appearance change?"

"Yes. His body is going to evolve to handle the power it

will hold. But I promise you, when it happens, your eyes will be blessed," Sheba giggled.

"I'm scared," I confessed.

"Don't be afraid of what you don't yet understand. Place your trust in your heart," Sheba said, placing her hand on my chest where my heart was located. "This will never steer you wrong."

Sheba gave me a hug and wished me well.

"Will I see you again?"

"No. Once you give yourself to Maahes, you won't be able to walk on these holy grounds. That is the reason the gentlemen were stopped just shy of the path. They are no longer pure although their love for you is sincere. But I will always be watching over you and your family," she smiled.

Sheba then pointed back to the trail that led me to her. As I got up and began to walk away, I could finally hear the birds chirping, the leaves rustling as the wind blew slightly, and the sound of the stream as it flowed quietly. I turned around to get one last glimpse of Sheba, but she was gone, along with her private oasis. All I could see was an old stone wall that looked as if it was about to crumble.

I made my way back to the steps and led the pack up them. When we reached the throne room, they had all morphed back into their human and had clothes on. None of them remembered going into the tomb but they all said that they felt closer to their beast. My father admitted that he saw life in a different light, and he felt that his senses had heightened.

"Well, I would love to hear more about your national geographic moment, but we have to hurry before the moon commences to bleeding. According to what the Almighty showed me, the Dark Prince and his misfit army will attack during the blood moon. The ceremony needs to be complete and we need to be ready for the fight of our lives," I told them.

"While the ceremony takes place, gather both packs and separate them into three teams," my father ordered.

"Juice, I need you to gather all our elderly and children and bring them to the temple. They will be safe from any harm here. Fisheth Zenunim agreed to place a secondary spell of protection on the temple and the Portal of Life to keep anyone outside of our pack or pride from entering," Pax announced.

"Stewart and Joker, I need one of you to bring Lucas

to the cathedral and the other one needs to bring Rouge. During the ceremony, I need both of you to guard the doors. We don't think we will have any problems, but just in case shit flies south with this Maahes character, I want both of you to be close by," my father stated.

I have never seen so many people move so fast. The warriors were gearing up, guards were ushering children and elderly into the temple, spells were being cast, and the cathedral was being prepared for the arrival of my twin flame. With the sun setting quickly, we were in a race to get battle ready.

Lilith helped me to prepare myself for the ceremony. She enjoyed standing in for my mother who couldn't physically be there. However, I was happy to know that she was given the opportunity to look down from Seventh Heaven as I entered another phase of my life.

Lilith pulled my hair up into a high ponytail and lined my face with angelic spiral curls. She wasn't a fan of make-up; stating that true beauty is natural. But she did allow me to accent my face with a soft brown eyeliner and a glittery pink gloss.

I was then helped into a sheer, white robe with golden accents. It left nothing to the imagination. My body was on display for all to see. You would think that I would be used to nudity as much as I see the males as they morph between their human and beast, but I wasn't. No one except my parents have had the pleasure of seeing my body; even then, I was only a small child. Then it hit me. Maahes is going to enter my body in the presence of my father! *Oh my god!*

Agrat bat Mahlat prepared the cathedral by decorating it with my favorite flower, the Stargazer lily. All around the cathedral were candles, emanating the soft scent of jasmine and in the background, I could hear the soft sound of a piano. The scene alone would make one fall deep in love.

I was led to the altar by my father where I saw Rouge sleeping peacefully. I stood on one side of the altar looking down onto the man who swooped into my life and stole my heart. I loved him so much. So, before the ceremony began, I leaned over to him and kissed him gently on his lips and said, "I promise my heart to you. There will never be another because the Almighty has created you just for me. Although I have power, your love is my weakness. I am powerless without you standing at my side. Together we are one, and we are strong. I promise to not only be the wife you desire, but the wife you need. I will be submissive, supportive, and bear you many children to carry out your legacy. I give my heart to you – forever and always. These were and still are my vows to you."

"Let's get started," Lucas announced.

I stood up with tears racing down my face and nodded my head for him to begin.

He started with a bible verse from Song of Solomon:

"Set Maahes as a seal upon your heart, as a seal upon your arm, for love is strong as death, jealousy is fierce as the grave. Its flashes are flashes of fire, the very flame of the Almighty. Many waters cannot quench love, neither can floods drown it."

Lucas then opened the box and began to pray over it. At times he held it high over his head while other times he sprinkled blessed waters over it. When he handed the Blade of Courage over to Samael and he whispered a few words to it, what was once a rusty, ancient knife; had transformed into a gorgeous, shiny, jewel encrusted dagger.

The blade was then handed to me so that I could insert it into Rouge's chest. Before taking the life of the man I loved, I looked around for Pax. I knew this was breaking every inch of his heart and there was nothing I could do to mend it.

His eyes were red, and I could see his tears slowly streaming down his face. Pax had other sons, but Rouge was his number one. This was the only child of his that followed directly in his footsteps. This man has lost his daughter, killed his wife, and now I was taking his son away. How much should one person have to endure?

I turned back to focus my attention on Rouge as he peacefully slept. Then, I raised my arms to the Heavens, with the blade securely held with both of my hands and plunged it down forcefully into Rouge's chest.

I was expecting for the earth to quake, see his blood gush out of his chest like a fountain, or hear the loud rumbling of thunder; but there was nothing. Just an awkward silence that filled the cathedral.

Pax walked up to the altar and pushed me slightly aside. He stood there for a few seconds just looking at his son as his body lay motionless. He took his hands and placed them onto his chest and then placed one hand on top of his. Pax didn't speak a word. He just stood beside his son with his head held high.

Samael then touched Rouge's body and the Blade of Courage disintegrated with its ashes evaporating into the air. Before Samael touched Rouge's body, we could not see any rise or fall of his chest and his skin had turned a pale grey.

After his subtle touch and hearing him say the words, "Awaken, son of Ra and Bastet; God of War and Protection, and twin flame of Serenity. You have slept long enough, Warrior of Alexandria."

Rouge's skin slowly turned an eye-catching shade of chestnut, his body thickened as his muscles were chiseled and carved to perfection, his hair was long, straight, and jet black, and when he opened his eyes and looked at me, I instantly became lost in his spirit. Those captivating hazel eyes with hints of gold made my heart skip a beat with excitement.

Rouge sat up and looked around the room as if it was the first time he had visited the cathedral. As he hopped down from the altar, he looked at his father for a second and then pulled him in for a hug. "I'm still here old man. Quit crying like a bitch and give me some love," he joked with him.

"Rouge?" I asked softly.

He looked in my direction and began to analyze my being. As I took a step toward him, he took one towards me. I raised my hand and placed it on his cheek as I searched for the man I loved. Rouge wrapped his arms around my waist and pulled me to him. He dipped his head and planted the softest, sweetest kiss on my lips. "I'm still here," he whispered. "I'm still here."

"My Lord," Lucas said. "Is all forgiven?"

When Rouge turned his attention to Lucas, I could see the change in him. The way he walked, the words he chose, and his display of power, told me that Maahes had emerged.

"You mean to tell me that you're still alive?" Maahes huffed.

"Of course, My Lord. I have been anxiously awaiting your return. I even offered my body to be a vessel," Lucas answered, as he bowed to Maahes.

Maahes made his way around to the other side of the altar and looked down onto Lucas. As rage danced in his eyes, he plunged his hand deep into Lucas's chest and withdrew it;

holding the heart of his betrayer in his tight grasp. It happened so quickly that Lucas was watching his heartbeat in Maahes' hand for several seconds before his body fell to the floor.

"As heartbroken as we all are about Lucas's demise, I need you to bond with your wife. We have a battle to attend," Samael said slyly.

He dropped Lucas's heart onto the floor and focused his energy on me. With his eyes locked on my essence, he slowly made his way back to where I was standing. Maahes gently pushed his father out of his way and stood close in front of me. With my heart pounding violently against my chest with anticipation, he dropped to his knees. He lifted my robe to my hips and buried his nose deep into my sweet spot. Maahes inhaled several long breaths before flickering his tongue across my tingling numb. As he roared loud enough to wake the dead, my body shivered in fear, but my sweetness leaked profusely.

"Serenity," he whispered. "Will you surrender your heart to me?"

"You have always held my heart within your hands, My Love," I answered.

I could feel as he used his finger to explore my blessed garden, inserting it deep into its well. The warmth and length of it made my body quiver in need.

As he pulled his finger out slowly and inserted it into his mouth, he moaned in ecstasy.

"Allow me to help her onto the table," Samael offered.

"No," he answered harshly. Instead, Maahes took me by my hand and led me out of the cathedral. "I will never shame you by taking your body in a manner that isn't fit for a queen."

We made our way through the city to a large building that sat along the Nile. Although I had seen this building multiple times, I had never really paid it any attention. When Maahes chanted a couple of words in his ancient tongue, the building looked as if it had just been built. He waved his hand and the double doors opened widely exposing a gorgeous open room with large windows that gave us a stunning view of the Nile.

Followed by my father and his entourage, the elders, and Pax, we entered Maahes' home. "I ask that you grant me and my new wife some privacy so that we may consummate our marriage."

"But it needs to be witnessed," Samael stated.

"Then only one of you will be allowed. Since Serenity is directly tied to Lilith, and she is an elder, it will be her who I grant access into our bedroom," Maahes stated.

"As you wish, Maahes," Samael agreed. "Just remember that time isn't on your side this night."

Maahes nodded his head and pulled me through our new home and up to our new chambers. When we reached our room, he opened the door for me and watched as my eyes lit up with joy as they were greeted by the luxurious furnishings and décor. Our bedroom was decorated with a huge bed with large white pillows, a plush comforter, and an exquisite view of the Nile.

"Did I meet your expectations, My Angel?"

I couldn't even answer him because I was too busy throwing myself into his arms and showering him with kisses. Soon, those grateful kisses turned into passionate advances. As our tongues became intertwined, Maahes lifted my body up and carried me over to our bed.

He stood on the side of it and removed his robe and

then leaned over to me and graciously helped me out of mine. As I sat on the side of the bed, he ran his finger down the side of my face, down my neck, and to my hardened nipples, where he took his time to circle them.

With the moon beginning to reveal itself, I scooted backwards onto the bed, laid on my back and waited for him to join me. Slowly, he crawled into the bed, with his hardness standing at attention, and laid between my welcoming thighs. He kissed me softly on my lips and whispered that he loved me. Feeling his masculine body as it laid on mine made my blood warm with want.

Maahes grabbed his manhood and slowly began to push inside of my sweetness. As he gradually inched himself into my blessed gardens, I gasped at the sensation of it stretching me open to its limits. There was no room for error as it snuggly rested halfway inside of me.

"You are incredibly tight but warm and wet," he moaned.

Leisurely, he started to thrust into my body with sensual and precise movements. Passionately pushing in and gradually pulling out. With the sharp pains fueled with pleasure, I wrapped my legs around his waist and began to match his rhythm. As my wetness adjusted to his girthy pipe, he was deep within me, flexing his muscles with each obsessive stroke.

I was enjoying him now. I loved the way he held me close to his body and showered me with kisses. I was intoxicated with the scent of his soft vanilla scent and seduced by his soft but masculine moans. I could feel as our heartbeats synced and our spirits united. I felt safe and secure wrapped in his arms. And when I looked into his eyes as he made love to me, I fell deep into euphoria. Sheba was right, we were connecting on a level that satisfied my mind, body, and soul.

Enjoying every inch of his hardness, I moaned in pleasure. I could feel as his manhood pulsated inside of me, as his body warmed with lust, and his body thrusted fervently to a moderate tempo.

My moans were now cries of desire with lust exciting every nerve in my body. Maahes was working overtime as he pounded viciously into my sweet spot. My body started to tremble, my heart was thumping violently, and my body was screaming out in pleasure.

"I'm close!" he yelled.

I couldn't answer him because I was on the brink of my climax. He was destroying my walls and pulverizing my g-spot. My cream was flowing like lava as he pushed me over the edge, and I collapsed into ecstasy.

"Shhhhit!" he yelled, as his body jerked fiercely.

I held him close as his body continuously shook, and his manhood throbbed aggressively inside of me. As his body calmed, he buried his head deep into the crease of my neck as he gave thanks to the Almighty for this union.

Lilith made her way to the side of our bed and slid her hand between our sweaty bodies. She smiled wickedly and announced to us that my egg had been fertilized.

"Are you going to take my first born?" I questioned.

"No. I cannot take the child of a god," she explained.

"Is it a boy or girl?" Maahes asked.

"Serenity is pregnant with your son. Congratulations Maahes," she said as she shimmered out of our chambers.

"I pledge my life to you and our family. Both families," he said, slowly pulling out of me. "I just need a few minutes to regain my strength and then I will be ready to face my brother."

"And what if Lei is there?" I asked. Mating with Maahes one time had me addicted to him. I was craving more of his hardness like a crackhead to her crackpipe.

"She too can meet the sharp edge of my blade, along with my brother's unborn son," he replied.

~~~~~~~~~~~~~~~~~~~~~~

Chapter Thirteen

The War – Gethambe

We split our soldiers into three parts. I would lead one, Pax would lead the second one, and Maahes would lead the third one; if I can get him to focus on something else besides my daughter. I understand the whole twin flame thing, but we are in the midst of a war. Maahes needs to calm his sexual desire for Serenity until after the battle is won.

Although Samael and Lilith cannot participate in the war, they have agreed to teleport Pax's crew behind Lucifer's camp. Eisheth Zenunim shielded their being with a cloaking spell so that Lucifer will not be able to sense their presence until it's too late and they had already attacked them from the rear.

Maahes and Serenity will teleport the third team to the west of the enemy. There is nothing that can shield Maahes' being from his brother or Serenity's scent from Lana. But with the amount of power they have surging through their beings, I'm not the least bit worried about them. The only thing that we are all unsure of is how Abrey intends to use that damn philosopher's stone. Maahes will be unaffected by it, but Serenity could fall victim and lose all her powers. However, Maahes has given me his guarantee that my daughter will be safe in his charge.

After the other two teams were in place, and the moon turned an amazing crimson red, the gatekeeper sounded the horn and the gates to Alexandria were opened. Moving as one unit, we marched together using our shields to form a wall. When we were just shy of the forest, the Canine Crew parted their shields like the Red Sea, allowing me to take the lead.

Although they were quiet, I could smell the cowards that were hiding behind the tall trees and thick scrubland. With my army standing behind me, I yelled out to them, "Show your face!" And like the wild dogs that they were, the Aamons came rushing out by the hundreds but stopped just shy of a few hundred feet from where I stood.

They were enraged and thirsty for our blood. They were howling and fighting amongst themselves like untamed mongrels as we stood steady and strong. The pride and the pack were a furious, disciplined group of warriors who weren't easily rattled. Not even with all the commotion and noise of our enemy that tried desperately to show their strength.

As I analyzed our situation, the demonic Lana appeared. It had been so long since I had seen her that I forgot how amazingly beautiful she was. Pregnancy had a way of showcasing her finest qualities. Lana's skin was a smooth cooper tone that glowed under the blood moon, her frame was small with curves in all the right places, but her eyes were dark and filled with hatred.

"Gethambe, My Love," she said. "I'm so happy to see you. Will Ashley be joining us on this festive occasion?"

"Lana," I smiled. "Ask your new husband how it feels to have my sloppy seconds?"

"Still the arrogant asshole, I see," she answered as she closed the gap between us. "At least with my new husband, he is able to fill me up and fulfill my needs. I don't have to worry about little things anymore."

"Now we both know I'm far from little. This anaconda had your scrawny ass on bedrest for many days," I laughed.

I could see that I had just tickled her nerve because her eyes began to twitch, and her smile turned into a frown. Instead of responding, she just said softly, "Kill them all."

Lana disappeared as quickly as she surfaced.

As they charged towards us, I pulled out my Bae and steadied my attack stance. Moving simultaneously, my first line of defense pulled out their swords and positioned themselves for battle. When the first Aamon made contact, I pushed my blade deep into his chest and watched as his body exploded.

Then, I slowly made my way through the crowd, followed by my soldiers, slashing the enemies and watching as their bodies disintegrated to ash. I swung my Bae viciously, twisted and turned my body with military precision; desperately trying to find an end to the massive army that attacked us.

It seemed as if we had been in this battle for hours and there were more Aamons charging us. The more we killed, the more the Jinn created. At one point in time, it seemed as if my body was moving in slow motion and I was just standing there counting the bodies of my kin. It angered me that so many of my people would ascend into Valhalla this night.

Enraged with the number of Canine soldiers and Lionesses that lay motionless on the ground, I threw my sword to the side and morphed into my beast. I had my sights set on the Jinn but had an appetite for Lana's blood. Although I'm not a baby killer, I knew in my heart that I was going to dispose of that bitch for once and for all. Lana needed to pay for all the blood she had a hand in spilling.

I ran as if I had cheetah blood coursing through my veins. My movements were so swift that my surroundings became a blur. I homed my eyes in on my target and leaped high into the air. As my body began to come back down, I extended my claws and sliced the Jinn into three equal parts. But his body mended itself back together and he spun around in circles and laughed as if I tickled his soul.

It was then that I realized that I needed the assistance of Serenity or Maahes. I didn't know how much energy I had left in my body to continue this fight. And as I looked at my loyal soldiers, I didn't know how much longer they could sustain the constant attacks. Everyone was beginning to look so exhausted.

The War – Maahes

Before we were to attack my brother and his minions,

I wanted to give my wife something special. I was warned by Lilith that the Dark Prince was in possession of the philosopher's stone and he planned on using it to cipher my wife's powers.

I stood behind Serenity and wrapped my arms around her waist. I pulled her back to me and squeezed her body gently. I kissed her on the side of her neck and then whispered in her ear.

"Do you trust me?" I asked her.

"Of course, I do," she smiled, as she leaned her head backwards on to me.

I then used my nail to cut my wrist and asked her to drink my blood. "I need you to do this for me; for us."

She pulled away from me and looked at me with terror in her eyes. I could tell that she didn't know where I was going with this and didn't really quite trust me.

"You want me to drink you blood?" she questioned.

"Yes. And then I want you to allow me to drink yours," I said to Serenity.

She stood there for a couple of seconds before grabbing my arm and wrapping her soft, plush, sexy lips around my wrist. She slowly sucked the blood my wound and swallowed it without hesitation.

As she digested my blood, her skin brightened, her eyes changed to an amazing turquoise color, and her tight curls straightened. She looked up at me and then around at the forest. I watched as her smile lit up the night, shining brighter than the blood moon. Her innocent, naïve, personality was adorable.

"I can hear, feel, and see everything. I can hear the ants as they scatter about in their colony, I can feel the presence of my ancestors, and I can see everything clearly for miles. What did you do to me?" she asked softly. She was becoming aroused to her new abilities.

"You are officially bonded to me. My blood is now your blood. Everything that I am, you are. And after I drink from your wrist, I will be officially bonded to you."

My blood will protect her against the philosopher's stone. I couldn't imagine losing her although our journey together just begun. Everything about her being draws me into her.

"Your turn," she smiled angelically.

Serenity used her nail to slit her wrist and held it up high for me to drink from it. I grabbed her by the arm and wrapped my lips around her tiny wrist and digested a part of her sweet essence.

If Lucifer didn't know before now that I was there, he knew now. When I pulled away from Serenity, I expelled a thunderous roar. It was so loud that it vibrated the ground beneath our feet. I looked at my wife and pulled her close to me and gave her a passionate kiss.

"You are now bonded to me officially, Maahes," she grinned.

"We are one," I said. "Are you ready?"

"Let's wreak some serious havoc on the demonic souls of the Underworld," she replied; allowing me to lead our people into battle.

When we approached the opening to where my brother and his wife sat as they watched the battle, I was overcome with rage. They sat there with their heads held high as if they knew this was a war they were assured. They didn't expect the unexpected…that my spirit would be released, and I would be joined with Serenity.

As soon as we emerged from the dense woods, my brother eyes filled with rage. My body had changed but he could still see my soul. I looked over to see Gethambe who had exhausted himself as he fought heroically, killing as many Aamons as he and his team could handle.

"Serenity," I said. Because we were one, I didn't have to say another word. She knew what I needed her to do and she ran at top speed to execute my orders.

With the clan behind her, taking up the slack from Gethambe's initial attack, she tossed demons left and right until she reached her father. I, on the other hand walked into battle slowly, absorbing the souls of my brother's minions. One by one, I inhaled their spirit which fueled my being. Each one igniting my fire and charging my beast.

After inhaling several hundred of them, my deity emerged. My angel stood eight feet tall, my body was nicely chiseled, and my white wings with gold accents were enormous.

I had all my brother's attention. He instantly stood up and allowed his demon to surface. As I started towards him, my brother couldn't help himself by throwing a rabbit into the hat. He summoned Lei and she was just as beautiful as the day I had laid eyes on her so many decades ago.

"Maahes," she said, as she started towards me. "It's been a long time."

With the battle raging around us, the bitch sitting on her throne that I wanted so desperately to kill, and that slithering snake Abrey making his way towards my wife; Lei made it hard to focus on which issue was more important. Her presence was clouding my judgement.

"Its okay to love her," I heard Serenity whisper. "But remember that she is your past and I am your future. I am your twin flame. The only being in these realms that can control your beast and satisfy your spirit while fulfilling your beast."

I know my brother wasn't expecting my next action, but as Lei got within reach of my nails, I extended them and slashed her throat. I loved her, but I realize that she has never loved me. Besides, since my brother has been wading in her waters, that whore smelled of deceit and misery.

"Now handle your business while I handle Lucifer's nut sack," Serenity said.

I kicked Lei's body to the side and started for Lucifer. I had grown tired of his lust for power. He had a whole world that he created and dominated, why did he feel like he was entitled to more?

He stepped down from his throne and stood face to face with me. His broken heart held no fear, and my heart held no regrets. It was time for us to end this war and time for him to return to that desolate place he called, his kingdom.

The War – The Mad King Abrey

I could tell that we were losing this war. We have been hit by two separate teams and I know there was another one hidden to our rear. This should have been an easy win for us, but that silly Jinn that I sent to spy for me gave them all the ammo they needed to get prepared. I should have known better.

Lucifer's bitch ass ain't even participating. He has his nose so far up Lana's ass that he can't lead his army. He allowed that whore turned housewife to run the show. I can't believe this nigga is going that hard for a piece of ass.

Gethambe's soldiers are well-trained, and I knew that

coming into this battle. That's why I had six Jinns creating Aamons constantly. They may be efficient killers, but how long can they hold out? Because they are exhausted, they are starting to make mistakes and I love it. Soon, he won't have any soldiers left to fight for him, and that is when I will step in and take over all that he loves. Hell, I might even trade Cherish's ass in for Ashley. She has the ability to produce the best seeds. Together, we could conquer all twelve realms.

As Maahes' faces off with his brother, I now have Serenity in my sight. Once I cypher her powers, I'm going to ease my way over to where my precious daughter is sitting on her throne and cypher hers as well. This shit is like taking candy from a baby.

I ignited the philosopher's stone by saying the incantation that my daughter taught me. As it burned cherry red, I needed to get close enough to Serenity for it to start the transfer. Because she is busying herself by attacking my Jinns and sucking the souls from the demons who are attacking her clan, she won't even see me coming.

As I inched up close to where she stood, and waited for the philosopher's stone to kick in, she turned and locked eyes with me. By now she should be feeling the effects of becoming powerless, but her powers were still at full strength. So, I chanted the incantation again thinking that I said something incorrect, but to my dismay, it still wasn't pulling from her. What the fuck is going on? What type of trickery witchcraft has Eisheth Zenunim provided her with?

"Pretty rock," Serenity said sarcastically.

Okay, so I may not be able to suck her body dry of its enlightened well, but I was still not one for her to fuck with.

"You knew?" I laughed.

"That you want to steal what doesn't belong to you?" she smiled mischievously.

"You don't deserve the power your body possesses."

"And you do?" she snapped. Before I could get close to her, Gethambe appeared. But being the bitch she was, Serenity extended her arm and held him back.

"All I need is two seconds to rip his head from his body and shove it up his ass. I owe him a swift and painful death for killing his own son," Gethambe huffed. His chest swelled as his voice rattled my spine.

"No," Serenity said. "I got this. Help the pack and

Canine Crew while I end his existence."

Gethambe craved my blood the way I craved Serenity's powers. Everything about his being said so. But he was a good boy and listened to his daughter.

"I'm no match for a creature as powerful as you," I said to her. "But riddle me this before you dissolve my essence into the great unknown. How are you immune to the philosopher's stone?"

"Because you cannot take the power of a god," she answered simply, as she wrapped her ponytail up into a tight knot.

"You may have god-like powers, Serenity. But you are no god."

"Right before the war, my husband allowed me to drink from him as he drank from me. Our souls are united, and our powers are equal," she answered, as she slowly circled me.

"Awe," I smiled. "You are a god by default. So smart of Maahes," I chuckled.

"No powers," she said to me. "Hand to hand combat."

Now she was speaking my language. This is what I

did. I trained soldiers for many decades. So, fighting this little pussycat wasn't shit.

When she came face to face with me, she charged forward and turned her back to me as she slammed her elbow into my face. Immediately, blood spurted from my nose and mouth simultaneously. I shook it off and caught her in mid-spin and punched her in the face.

My blow didn't seem to faze her, and she charged me again. This time, she lifted her leg, pulled it back to her chest, and powerfully lunged it forward, landing directly in the center of my chest. The impact was so potent that I'm sure my heart stopped beating for a second or two. My body flew into a tree and before I could recuperate, she charged forward, held me by my neck, and power-drove her fist into my face multiple times.

With every impact of her fist, my spirit began to dim. However, I wasn't done. Right as she used her knee to kick me in the stomach, I flung her body around and used my elbow to plant a blow onto her face. Then I grabbed her by the arm and tossed her body over my back and threw it down onto the ground. I ran over to her and violently began to stomp my heel into her chest.

She grabbed my foot, twisted it left and then right, and I could feel every bone in my ankle snap, crackle, and pop. Serenity then pulled it towards her making my body slam against the ground. As my body made contact, blood spurted from my mouth like a fountain.

I was coughing and in pain, but I still had the heart of a lion and my fight instinct was strong. I tried to roll over and get to my feet, but Serenity wasn't giving me any leeway. She continuously kicked me back down to the ground.

When she grew tired of toying with her prey, she straddled me and sat on my chest. She looked deep into my soul and said, "You took the best part of me, from me. My father was my world, the only person who truly understood me besides my mother," she said with tears in her eyes.

"Bullet wasn't no son of mine. He lacked the heart of a warrior and settled for being a bitch to that whore. Gethambe had a better chance of being favored by me," I huffed, as I spat up blood.

She couldn't handle the truth about her beloved, Bullet. Serenity lifted my head, twisted it quickly to the right, and snapped my neck. Because I was already sentenced to hell, my soul would cease to exist. There is no afterlife for me.

The War – Serenity

I watched as Abrey's body turned to ashes and then focused my attention back on the battle of our lifetime. I grew tired of watching my friends and family fall to a senseless war. Before taking Abrey's life, I saw that Lana and Lucifer didn't want any part in this. This whole battle had to do with Abrey's obsession with me and the power he would never possess.

I felt a surge of power racing through my body as I ended his pathetic life. So, I found my way back to the battlefield where Pax and his team had arrived. They were doing a marvelous job taking down the thousands of Aamons, but I could do it quicker with minimal life loss.

As I walked through the mindless drones that continuously fought against my clan, I thought of death and destruction. When I focused on a group of demonic entities, they exploded. Hundreds at a time, I was sending them back to the depths of Hell.

I scanned the area to find the last Jinn that was creating these beasts as quickly as I could kill them. When I finally located him, I saw that he was being protected by none other than Lana. Now it was time for big bank to take little bank. This bitch wasn't ready.

I started toward where she sat high on her throne with every intention of ripping Lucifer's heart from her chest. But she was pregnant with my brother and he was an innocent bystander in this war. Being pregnant myself, I couldn't take this from her. Not even after all the hell she has caused.

When I approached her temporary throne, my blood boiled with rage. She didn't have the protection of her husband because he was in a bitter battle with his brother. So, she had to deal with me on her own.

"Either lower your shield and allow me to kill that Jinn, or I will forget that you are pregnant and rip your heart from your body," I demanded.

"Silly child," she laughed. "Tricks are for kids. I am just as powerful as you. Don't let this belly fool you. Unlike Ashley, my pregnancy doesn't weaken my powers."

Since she was from the show me state, I figured I

should give her an example of who she was really fucking with. I have grown as an enchantress and have gained more power than I know what to do with. Lana was in for the surprise of her life.

With the wind blowing through my hair, the power emanating from my body, and the spells taught to be by an original, it only took me a second or two to dismantle her shield. Then, I stood in the atomically position with my arms down to my side, slightly away from my body, with my palms facing forward. I said another incantation to set the Jinn on fire and dissolved his being. My palms glowed a serene white as lightning shot forcefully from them.

As the lightning made impact with the Jinn, his body flamed up and he began to yell in excruciating pain. His body spun fiercely around in circles before being sucked into the ground. Lana's eyes were filled with fear as she grasped her stomach. She knew that I was pissed, and she was next on my list.

"Sit," I yelled. Her body was pushed backwards and thrown into her throne. I walked up to her and looked deep into her tormented soul and compelled her to not move. "You will sit here quietly until I return. You will not use your magic or summon any demons. You will not assist your husband as he fights his brother. The only thing you can do, is watch as I slaughter every demonic soul your Jinn created."

I left her sitting in her throne, dazed. I then made my way to the battle that continued to rage on. I walked slowly through the massive crowd of demons and stopped when I reached the center. I held my head down and extended my arms out. As my body levitated off the ground, it spun slowly until I gathered enough energy from my ancestors to send out a gigantic blast to kill any demonic entity still fighting.

As the surge of power rippled throughout the land, Aamon after Aamon met their demise. The ground shook, trees were uprooted, and the wind blew aggressively as it twirled like a tornado. Nothing demonic was left standing with the exception of Lucifer and Lana.

When my body lowered, and I opened my eyes, I could see the relief on the faces of my friends and family. Their bodies were so tired that their bodies fell to the ground as quickly as their swords.

"No more death!" I yelled out. "No more fighting," I

said, looking at my husband and his brother.

Maahes' body was still fueled with rage. He hated that his brother had killed his son and lived the life of a king while his soul was imprisoned. So, when he knocked Lucifer to the side, he immediately went for Lana. With nothing standing in his way, and her unable to fend for herself because I had compelled her not to move, he went for the kill.

Before he reached Lana, I shimmered over to her and stood strong and ready to fight my husband.

"What are you doing?" he asked.

"I will not let you kill her unborn son," I said to him.

"I'm due this justice," he demanded.

"In order to kill her and that child, you are going to have to kill me."

"With all the wrong she has done to you, you're still willing to forgive her?" my father said as he made his way to me.

"I don't condone her actions, but she carries my brother in her womb. This is not his fight and it's not his fault that Lucifer took my husband's first born. We are not the Almighty and cannot pass judgement," I said.

Lucifer walked up to me and dropped to his knees. I could see in his eyes that he truly loved Lana and that he loved his son. He may not feel bad for killing his brother's son, but he surely didn't want us to take the life of his.

"Get them out of my sight," Maahes huffed.

"As you wish, My Love," I answered him. "Lucifer take your wife and unborn child back to Hell. You will never return topside again, or you will forfeit your son's life and I will petition for the Almighty to take Lana's," I told him.

"So, you forgive me?" Lana asked.

"My heart tells me I have to forgive you. But I will never forget all the wrong you have done. I will never acknowledge you as my mother and I don't ever want to see your face again," I said to her, but not giving her the satisfaction of me looking in her direction.

"And what about your brother?" she asked. "Are you going to condemn him for my sins?"

"I will love him with all my heart until he decides that he will come for my soul. On that day, he too will meet his demise and be sentenced to Hell for all eternity."

With that being said, Lucifer took his wife and

shimmered them back to the Underworld. I placed a spell on the portal they used to come topside, prohibiting any other demon from entering our realm.

We gathered our dead heroes and prepared them for their peaceful journey into Valhalla.

As the sun rose on the new day, we began to heal.

~~~~~~~~~~~~~~~~~~~~~~~~~~~~

Epilogue

With Lana condemn to Hell, bitter took over her heart. After giving birth to her son, she vowed to seek revenge on Serenity for publicly shaming her when she tried to ask for forgiveness. With the support of her husband, Lana began to teach her son all the ways of the dark arts. Although he was born a demon, in the eyes of the Almighty, he was still an innocent because his life was unblemished.

Ashley returned to Alexandria but left to rule Achaemenid with Gethambe. They ruled their kingdom as equals and stopped many of the traditions that separated the people. Zira, Malik, and Dion were taught the ways of both clans and were in constant training to become rulers of their own great nation.

Ashley and Gethambe decided that since Lance was to become the protector of Alexandria and Jericho, when he was old enough, he would start his training with the Canine Crew. He would not only spend much of his day with them, but he would also spend time with Serenity. It was important for him to bond with his sister and her husband since they found out that their first born would be a great warrior as well. The only difference between the two was that Serenity's son would be fueled with magic.

Maahes learned to let go of all the hate that he held in his heart for his brother. With the help of Serenity, he was able to forgive him and understood that being evil was just in his nature. He knew that there would come a time that his children would have to stand against his brother's children, but until that time arrived, he allowed his hatred to lie dormant deep within him.

The realms were all at peace for the time being. The people of both realms focused their energy on rebuilding their home and repopulating the clans. Both Serenity and Ashley decided that they were willing to add another clan to their families. They wanted to seek out the Siberian Tigers and offer them a home. They knew that there were more of them out there that had been shunned from the Almighty's graces. So, they both sent a small recovery team out to find them to let them know that they were welcomed to both cities.

Although the great battle has ended, you never know what the future could hold.

~~~~~~~~~THE END~~~~~~~~~

Message to the Reader

First, I would like to thank God for giving me the gift to write these stories. Without my faith in him, I would not flourish as an author or a person.

Secondly, I want to thank my husband, family, and Quiana Nicole for their continued support because without their time, patience, and understanding – I wouldn't be able to give you my best. So, to the man that I love with all my heart…Terence Derone Smith, I appreciate all that you do. Your generosity has not gone unnoticed.

Finally, I thank you…the readers! As a new author, I appreciate your willingness to ride with me on this journey. You guys are just simply amazing!

I hope you enjoy this series as much as I enjoyed writing it. Please leave a review and tell me what you think! Thank you from the bottom of my heart.

Keeping Up With Monica

www.eroticauthormlsmith@gmail.com

www.eroticauthormlsmith.com

https://twitter.com/AuthorMLSmith73

https://www.instagram.com/terrylynsmith/

https://www.facebook.com/authormonicasmith

https://www.facebook.com/terrylynsmith

Other Books by Monica L. Smith

Skinwalkers

Skinwalkers 2

Chasing Storm

Sins of a Housewife

Sins of a Housewife 2: The Hennessy Chronicles

Sins of a Housewife 3: Rekindled

Sinful Halloween: An Erotic Novella

Downloaded Desires: An Erotic Connection

Secret Deception

Be sure to <u>LIKE</u> our Major Key Publishing
page on Facebook!

CPSIA information can be obtained
at www.ICGtesting.com
Printed in the USA
LVHW041759010419
612563LV00003B/346

9 781798 887806